BRAZILIADA

SHERIDAN WEST

Wicked West Publishing

Wicked West Publishing
Vancouver BC

This book is a work of fiction. Names, characters, institutions, places, and incidents are either product of the author's imagination or are used fictitiously, and any resemblance to actual person, living or dead, business establishments, events, or locales is entirely coincidental.

ISBN 978-1-7773180-2-4 (hardcover) / ISBN 978-1-7773180-1-7 (paperback) / ISBN 978-1-7773180-0-0 (ebook)
Library of Congress Control Number: 2020914847

Edited by Kelly Reed
Cover design by Wicked West Publishing

Publisher's Cataloging-in-Publication Data
provided by Five Rainbows Cataloging Services
Names: West, Sheridan, author.
Title: Braziliada / Sheridan West.
Description: Vancouver, BC : Wicked West Publishing, 2020.
Identifiers: LCCN 2020914847 (print) | ISBN 978-1-7773180-1-7 (paperback) | ISBN 978-1-7773180-2-4 (hardcover) | ISBN 978-1-7773180-0-0 (ebook)
Subjects: LCSH: Young women--Fiction. | Politicians--Fiction. | Brazil--Fiction. | Bildungsromans. | Mystery fiction. | Suspense fiction. | BISAC: FICTION / Mystery & Detective / Amateur Sleuth. | FICTION / Mystery & Detective / International Crime & Mystery. | FICTION / Coming of Age. | FICTION / Thrillers / Suspense. | GSAFD: Mystery fiction. | Suspense fiction. | Bildungsromans.
Classification: LCC PR9199.3.W47 B73 2020 (print) | LCC PR9199.3.W47 (ebook) | DDC 813/.6--dc23.

wickedwest.org

CONTENTS

THE SPRING MORNING IN LATE September 1992 was beautiful and sunny. A young couple lucky enough to live in Itaim Bibi, one of the trendiest neighborhoods of São Paulo, exited the neatly gardened entrance of an apartment building. They approached a shiny new Fiat Punto parked at the curb nearby.

"Are you sure you can make it there safely, Priscilla?" the man, dressed in a singlet with trunks and slippers, asked his wife.

"Of course I'm sure. I wouldn't risk it otherwise." The slender girl with long blond hair put a hand on her visibly pregnant belly, accentuated by the sky-blue fitted satin dress, in a gesture she'd adopted recently.

"I know. I know. I'm just worried because you

look a bit pale. And honestly, I'm not happy that I have to make my trip to Lindageral without my favorite travel buddy tonight." The man sighed. "But I know that's no reason to make you linger in this stifling city while I'm at the meeting."

Priscilla chuckled. "Oh, Robert, you're so funny! It's just an hour-and-a-half trip, and you talk about it like it's a two-week journey across the ocean."

Robert unlocked the car and placed a travel bag in the trunk. "It still feels like an eternity without you by my side." He opened the driver's door for his wife and turned to kiss her goodbye.

"I know." Priscilla smiled. "Don't think that I miss you any less. I'm just tired of the city and want to get back to our garden and see how my seedlings are doing, sit under the orange tree, and start crocheting a coif for our baby. You can take the girl out of the village but not the other way around."

"I don't want to take anything out of you. You are just perfect the way you are." Robert looked at her with fondness and stroked her hair with his fingertips. "Be cautious on the road. I will come to you right after the meeting. See you soon, *carinho*!"

"Good luck at your meeting. I hope you get this contract!" said Priscilla, getting into the car. "Goodbye, carinho. don't make me wait for too long!" She started the engine and waved at Robert before departing.

Before seven in the morning, the streets of São Paulo were not yet flooded with traffic, so Priscilla quickly made her way out of the city to the highway leading north toward the state of Minas Gerais, where her husband's family estate was located in a small town called Lindageral.

Priscilla carelessly smiled at the light breeze on her skin from the open windows and the picturesque landscape along the way. She could never have imagined that she would have all this. Just a year and half before, she'd lived with her parents and two little brothers in a small village in the north of Minas Gerais, and after she finished school at the age of fifteen, her whole life was helping her parents raise cattle and cooking food that was instantly consumed by her ravenous brothers.

Everything changed one evening when a young and beautiful wanderer knocked on their gates and asked for help with his car, stalled on the roadside. While her father was busy connecting wires to jump-start the engine, Priscilla timidly questioned their guest about what brought him to their land. He looked and spoke in a way different from people she had seen before. His clothes were neat and pretty, and he smiled nicely at her and answered her questions despite her fear that he would simply ignore her as her father and other men did in most of the cases when she spoke to them. He said his name was Robert del Atore, he lived in São Paulo, and he was returning home after a business trip when his car failed him. He said something about his business— something to do with farm machinery—but she didn't quite understand those details at the time, charmed by the sound of his voice. She told him some incoherent story about a calf that had gotten lost the day before, with her and her brothers running all over the fields in search of it, and he listened and nodded.

A couple weeks later, he drove to their house again, that time on purpose, and invited her and her brothers to a cinema in Chapada Gaucha, the nearest big city, to thank them for helping him out. Many miles lay between São Paulo and her parents' house, but love knew no distance. Robert left her his phone number, but while he had the newest model of portable phone, their household didn't even have a landline, so she had to go to the neighbors' house to make a call. They talked every week, and the next time he came to their village, she left with him.

The handsome stranger was not just any commuter. At his twenty-four years, he ran Campoverde, one of the biggest companies selling agricultural machinery in all of Brazil. The company belonged to his family, which had also owned thousands of acres of coffee plantations in Saõ Paulo and Minas Gerais since the time of King Pedro.

Her family and all their neighbors could not believe what happened to her, but there she was, Senhora del Atore, Robert's wife and soon-to-be mother of his son.

She was taking a side road, the shortest way to the manor, located on the outskirts of Lindageral, when she noticed a heavy truck blocking her way. She stopped and honked a few times. Nothing happened. She waited a couple minutes then got out of the car.

At that moment, a scrawny gray-haired man dressed in a black suit stepped from behind the truck. "Hello, my darling. Now we meet at last." His tone promised nothing good. "Did you really think you could avoid me forever?"

Priscilla felt a hot flush of fear. Her heart pounded heavily in her chest, but she tried to keep her voice as steady as possible. "What is going on here, Don Amarillio? I thought we had settled everything with you. I promised you I would never say anything to Robert if you would leave me alone and treat me with respect as your son's wife."

The man laughed. "I really like the manner in which you get everything solved, my dear. What a demeanor! You really deserve more than my foolish son."

He approached her and stroked her face. Priscilla stepped back.

"What the hell are you doing?" A hint of panic slipped into her voice. "This time, I will have to tell Robert. This has gone too far!"

In the corner of her eye, she noticed two large men standing and watching, apparently Amarillio's bodyguards.

"Sorry, my dear, but no woman is allowed to say no to Amarillio del Atore. It will cost you."

He gestured to his men, and the two of them took her by her arms in a death grip before she could blink. Shocked and stunned, she stared at the gray-haired man, who was obviously reveling in her horror like a boa constrictor contemplating its hypnotized victim. He took a folding knife from his pocket and opened it with a click.

"I am really sorry, Priscilla. You are so beautiful and brave. You could have been my queen and had more than you could dream about. Now, you will perish for nothing."

He slowly moved the knife over her chest. A trickle of blood slowly ran down her breast, and her first thought was that her beautiful, expensive dress would be damaged. Then a new, devastating thought struck her: *Never mind the dress. I am going to be damaged or even killed right now, in this pretty blue dress, in the bloom of my youth. This man is crazy, and he won't let me live, never mind letting me go.*

"Please forgive me, Don Amarillio. I was stupid. I will do everything you say," she said with a dry mouth.

The man laughed, harsh wrinkles surrounding his cold blue eyes. "It's too late, my dear. I gave you many chances, but you discarded all of them."

Priscilla felt like her soul had already parted from her body. She looked at the scene as if it were not happening to her and she was just watching from the side. *This just can't happen. It's some crazy nightmare.* She desperately wished to wake up in her parents' house and find out the story was just a dream and Robert del Atore, son of one of the most dangerous and corrupt figures in the country, had never appeared at their doorway.

But obviously, it wasn't a dream, and she was standing before this man, and he was holding a knife in his hand. *What can I possibly do?* Thoughts were feverishly running through her head. *Say something. Reach out to him. Find the right words.*

"Don Amarillio, please! Robert will be heartbroken if something happens to me. Think about the baby! Your grandchild!"

The man's thin lips curved into a contemptuous sneer. "Maybe he will learn this way that he's still too weak to mess with me."

Priscilla choked and yelled at the top of her lungs, "Why do you hate your own son? Why you can't just leave us alone? What have we done to you?"

Ignoring her, Amarillio turned to his bodyguards, ignoring her screaming. "Light it up!"

One of them pushed the screaming Priscilla into her car while the other handed Amarillio a burning torch made of a stick wrapped in rags and soaked with gasoline. With a satisfied look, he threw the torch into the car through the open window.

CHAPTER ONE

AMELIA DEL ATORE WOKE UP BEFORE her smartwatch alarm set for seven in the morning went off. She closed her eyes again and lay in bed for several minutes, listening to the tweeting of birds and the rustling of leaves outside her window, feeling disoriented. In her dream, she'd been in São Paulo, making her way through a crowded city square with her friends. In São Paulo, her days started with the sounds of cars moving and honking down on the street, so waking up to the sounds of nature was something she still wasn't used to, even though it was pleasant.

When her parents decided to relocate to their country house in Lindageral, a town with a population of only ten thousand people, two months before, she wasn't happy to leave São Paulo, the city where she had spent most of eighteen years of her life. It seemed to have become a part of her identity, with its intense lifestyle, friends, and nightclubs, but her mother made a point of saying that while she enjoyed all the perks of having been born in del Atore's family, that came with its responsibility. Now, when her father, prominent business owner Robert del Atore, decided to put himself forward for the upcoming election to the Chamber of Deputies of São Paulo state, she and her mother had to do as much as they could to reinforce his good reputation. His living in a small town with his family and actively participating in the life of the local community, with his daughter attending public school, was the best demonstration of his being a decent and straightforward man, the one ordinary people would vote for.

Besides that, being away from the big city with its distractions and temptations definitely benefited Amelia's studying for her graduation exam, the ENEM, which she successfully passed in November, after which she and her classmates had one last month of classes before graduation.

In Lindageral, where the only entertainments available to her were a decrepit night club always filled with drunk and sweaty crowds, as well as a marketplace, a library, and a fitness club, the latter two were the only places she favored. She'd gone to the library once and gotten her card, but it couldn't compare to São Paulo's library, and although the librarian was a very interesting and friendly lady, Amelia was somewhat disappointed they didn't have the items she was looking for.

She also gave a local fitness club a try —she couldn't find a decent analog to her Brazilian jiujutsu classes and didn't want to lose her shape—but after the first time, when she felt quite uncomfortable under the greasy looks of its male attendants, she decided she was done being sociable and preferred to spend her free time in the comfort of her own home, which was newly renovated after being uninhabited for many years. After all, they had their own gym and library.

Amelia got dressed and went downstairs to the kitchen, where her mother was already cooking oatmeal for breakfast.

"Morning, Mom."

"Good morning, sweetheart," said Lucrecia, removing the steaming pot from the stove. "I was thinking how to better plan our time for tonight. When do your classes end today? At two, right?"

"Right."

"All right, then I will pick you up at two, and we will go to São Paulo right away. We should be there by four, and we will have some time to prepare for the soirée."

"Yes, sounds good. How many people will be there?"

"Twenty-five are invited, including the mayor of São Paulo and the governor. Believe it or not, it stresses me out. This will be a crucial moment for your father, so everything should be perfect." Lucrecia exhaled nervously and took a sip of coffee from a porcelain cup.

"Don't worry, Mom. It's not your first event with big bosses. I'm sure everything will be great."

"It must be. You won't need to stay there all the time and listen to all those boring conversations, but I would like you to help me by being the hostess of this event and making our guests notice what a well-mannered, smart, and sweet daughter your daddy has. It will definitely give him more points." Lucrecia winked at her.

Amelia gave an embarrassed chuckle "Mom! You definitely have a Machiavellian mind and will make an excellent gray cardinal. I think you should go to politics yourself. You could be our Hillary Clinton. I know she didn't win the presidency, but still..."

"No, thanks. I would rather be Cardinal Richelieu, if you like to draw analogies," retorted Lucrecia, and they both laughed.

After breakfast, Mother drove her to the school, which was about half an hour of walking distance from their house. Amelia used to ride a bicycle from time to time until it got stolen right from the school porch a few weeks before. She was in the classroom ten minutes before classes, and it was half empty. Her mate Charlotta, a girl with a cloud of curly hair, smiled and waved at her as she entered. Amelia smiled back and sat next to her.

A group of five guys at the back of the classroom were discussing something in a low tone. One of them stood and approached her.

"Morning, Amelia. How are you doing today?"

"Pretty good, thanks!" She smiled at him benevolently.

Marcelu was probably the only boy in her class she found pleasant. He was always neatly dressed and smelled of good deodorant and cologne, which made a drastic contrast with others, who wore lots of tasteless jewelry while not even bothering to take off their baseball caps indoors or change their clothes more often than once a week. And last but not least, he was able to maintain more meaningful conversation than "Yo, what's up, pretty!"

"Thank you so much for explaining logarithmic functions to me yesterday. You know I had a very hard time with it. Please take this with my gratitude," said Marcelu, handing her a small box styled like a Rubik's cube.

"Oh, thank you! What is this?"

She opened the lid, and a stream of water squirted her in the face.

Charlotta gasped in shock. Marcelu laughed and jumped back. The guys in the back seats burst into laughter. Amelia wiped her face with her palms and looked down at her white blouse, which had gotten soaked with water.

"Are you an idiot? What's wrong with you today?" she yelled at Marcelu, who quickly retreated from the classroom.

"Sorry about that, Am," said Charlotta. "Boys are all idiots. That's not funny at all!" she shouted, turning to the company at the back of the class.

"Yes, they are," agreed Amelia gloomily. "Even those successfully pretending to be normal people."

"Here, put this on." Charlotta took her cardigan from the back of her chair and handed it to her friend.

"Thank you. I hope I will dry out quickly."

"I think he's just trying to get your attention," whispered Charlotta.

"There are many better ways to do it. I'll be damned if I ever talk to him again."

She went outside to let her blouse dry in sunlight till the bell rang, and Charlotta followed her. To her dismay, Marcelu was roaming the schoolyard. She quickly looked away after their eyes met. Nevertheless, he approached them.

"Hey, Amelia. I do apologize. I know it was stupid, but I thought you would appreciate the joke," he said looking embarrassed.

"I am able to appreciate humor all right, but that was not a joke. That was offensive," she said dryly. "If you have such a small brain that you are not able to make normal jokes, then please refrain from it at all."

Charlotta gasped at the harsh reprimand and looked at Marcelu.

"Yes, you're right. No more jokes." Marcelu raised his hands apologetically. "What can I do to make it up to you? Can I ask you out to have a coffee with cake today?" He slyly squinted, his deep-blue eyes framed with long black lashes.

Amelia gave him a bewildered look, as if he were a box of rotten tomatoes somebody had offered to buy her at the marketplace.

"Listen. Maybe you consider yourself a great charmer, but all I see is an ill-mannered jerk. I'm not going anywhere with you, and no other girl with healthy self-esteem ever would. Now, please get out of my sight."

Marcelu shrugged and headed inside the school.

She passed him at a fast pace.

"Wow! That was brutal," commented Charlotta with a smirk.

"Hope it helps to keep him away." Amelia crossed her arms over her chest, still frowning.

"He's a good guy, though. Just acts like an idiot sometimes."

"I don't care how good he is. I want him to stay away until he learns to be respectful."

***

"Hey Robert, this meal was too damn good. I will never lose my weight if I keep visiting your house." Lando Lacerdo, a square man in his late fifties, leaned back in his chair and loosened his necktie.

The host of the soirée, a tall man with downy hair slightly touched with gray and with prominent cheekbones emphasizing his thinness, handed his guests shot glasses of rum and took his seat at a wide antique-style desk. "I'm glad you liked it. Lucrecia invited a chef from Estrella restaurant. I don't remember his name, but he's beyond competition."

His networking event went impeccably well. All the guests enjoyed the food, drinks, and conversation; some of them went to the spacious parquet-covered lounge with a glazed wall, to dance to the slow music; and pretty much all the figures of power promised Robert their support in the upcoming election.

After all the other guests left, Robert invited two of his friends and allies, Lando Lacerdo and Bruno Carvalho, to his home office for a drink or two. All three of them were successful middle-aged business owners who'd known each other for years, so Robert got straight to the point.

"My friends, Lando, Bruno, I appreciate that you found time to meet me and discuss our plan in detail." He opened a thick binder lying on his desk. "One of my good friends, Fabio Pedrosa, is a professor in the robotics department at the University of Campinas. Last year, the group of students he mentored developed something absolutely ingenious, which can potentially boost our economy if we do everything right."

He unfolded one of the papers and turned it toward his guests.

"Here are the technical drawings for the innovative construction of a coffee-bean-harvesting robot—they named it Harvey-3000. There were attempts to apply similar equipment in the field already, but we weren't happy with the results. But our Harvey employs an innovative machine-vision technology and other know-how, brilliant in its simplicity. We're trying to get a patent for it, but it will take a while, so I guess you understand that I expect you to keep this information strictly confidential. But it would be really great if we could start preparation for mass production of this machine in the meantime. And to do so would take all three of us working together."

Both of his buddies looked intrigued.

"I'm planning on using Lacerdo Motors facilities

for the production of the harvester. And your company, Bruno, could provide the electronic components."

Both of them nodded in understanding.

"I saw the prototype of Harvey in action, and it's really impressive. The problem with existing models is that they pick under- or overripe beans and add them to the bulk. This one employs special sensors to adjust its vibration parameters as it goes to pick only suitable beans. It's such a shame that, in the twenty-first century, we still have about seventy percent of coffee beans gathered manually—such a huge waste of human resources, let alone money. This machine can make drastic changes."

"Sounds impressive," said Bruno tentatively, "but are you sure that plantation owners will be ready to change their routine so quickly? You know, it's a very narrow niche, and risks are very high..."

"I know what you mean. But I'm sure that, provided with a proper presentation, they will be enthusiastic to apply it. Obviously, I will be the first to use these harvesters on my plantations. That would be the best advertising possible. Also, I'm friends with a couple of growers in Minas Gerais, and I discussed with them how great it would be to have some smart technology that could make the stressful and messy process of harvesting easier. Obviously, they would welcome any know-how that really works."

"May I take a look at this?" Lando Lacerdo took his reading glasses out of pocket and reached out for the assembly drawing.

Robert passed it to him.

For a couple minutes, Lando explored the huge sheet of paper. "Looks interesting," he said finally. "I would like to show it to my engineers and discuss with them."

"I'm not sure about that," Robert said cautiously. "As I mentioned, the invention is not patented yet, so I would prefer to keep the number of people who have access to the technical drawings as minimal as possible. Don't misunderstand me, but it will require such an extent of confidentiality that, even after we sign an agreement, I'll give you, Lando, drawings and schemes only for the mechanical parts, while Bruno will get only electronic schemes. But to make you understand how Harvey works, I will arrange a field trip for you both to see it in action."

"I definitely wouldn't discuss it with people I didn't know well, only with ones who have worked with me for many years. But if you want to keep total secrecy, I respect that," agreed Lando reluctantly.

"Well, it makes sense," said Bruno. "As they say, trust but verify. Some people are able to stay loyal only until the first serious temptation. And this"—he pointed at the folder—"has very good potential, I dare to suggest."

Lando nodded, not having much to say.

"I'm glad that you are both interested," resumed Robert. "As you understand, if I get elected into the Chamber of Deputies in October, I won't be able to be in charge of this project. So I presume that you, Lando, would take it over. And for my part, I will make sure all inspections and certifications will be passed without delays and procrastinations."

"Sounds good!" agreed Lando.

Bruno nodded. "I'm sure you will make it," he said. "Your party certainly will get enough seats, and you will get them. I'm sure São Paulo and Minas Gerais will favor you over the others. Who else from the locals can compete with you? Nestor Gomes, that old communist rat from the Labor Party and Leonardo Solas, who made his name with flash mobs on the internet? They don't stand a chance against you."

"Let's pray for that." Robert smiled.

***

After all the guests had left except for Senhors Lacerdo and Carvalho, Amelia went to the kitchen to get a piece of leftover tapioca pie and ate it without minding dinner etiquette. Her mother was there, chatting with their new housekeeper, Theresa.

"Did you enjoy the party, Amelia?" asked the gray-haired, dark-skinned woman.

"Yes, but I got a bit tired. So many guests—I was afraid I might have mistaken somebody's name."

"I know, sweetheart. It was stressful, but you did very well. And Theresa was just exceptional with all the arrangements," said Lucrecia. "I'm so happy to have found you, and thank you again, Theresa."

"It's my pleasure to help such a nice family, Senhora Lucrecia. Senhorita Amelia, I saw that you were dancing with that young man, Ramon, and I noticed how he looked at you and hung around you all night. I have to warn you about him. It's just between us and your mother, but this guy is really not good. I have friends who work for his family and heard some very bad things about him. You are such an innocent and sweet girl. You are a precious gem with a soul as clean as water in a mountain creek, but there are people who would take advantage of this. Forgive me, an old woman, for preaching, but you are dear to my heart."

"Good point," said Lucrecia, nodding.

"Thank you, Theresa." Amelia smiled, slightly confused. "No need to worry—I'm always aware. And I don't like that Ramon either. His charms don't work on me. Never liked macho men."

Saying that, she thought of Marcelu and his prank at school, which filled her with indignation again. Even he, whom she considered to be an adequate person, had turned to typical macho behavior.

He must have been a complete moron if he thought that would get her favor and attention, thought Amelia as she went upstairs to her bedroom. From then on, he would no longer exist for her. She wouldn't even say hello to him at school. She kept saying that to herself as she fell asleep in her bed.

After the long and eventful day, her sleep was troubled and shallow, and she quickly woke up when she heard a noise through the wall, from her father's office. Her first thought was that her father was still awake and working. But then she recognized the sound of a dial on the safe being turned multiple times.

A surge of adrenaline ran through her blood as the realization hit her: It could have been a robber trying to break into her dad's safe. And she was alone in pajamas in her bedroom.

Amelia took her cell phone from the bedside table and typed 190, preparing to call the police.

"Who's there? Dad, is it you?" she yelled.

The noise stopped abruptly.

"Who is it? I'm calling the police!"

She heard an indistinct noise then a loud *thud* outside, and she rushed to the window just in time to see a figure jumping off the patio roof below and running away. Wondering if her parents had heard the noise, she went to their bedroom, farther down the hall, and knocked frantically.

"Mom, Dad, wake up! We're being robbed!" Not waiting for a response, she burst in.

Her half-awake parents were sitting in their bed.

"What's going on? Are you all right?" Robert quickly rose to his feet and approached her.

"Dad, someone just was in your office, tampering with the safe, and then jumped out the window. I saw it with my own eyes!"

Her parents exchanged worried looks.

"I'll go check on it," said Robert.

"All right, I'll call the police in the meantime." Lucrecia took her cell phone from the nightstand.

Amelia followed her father to his office. The window was wide open, as was the door of the cabinet containing the safe, but the safe itself was closed. Robert hurried to unlock and inspect it.

"It looks like they tried to break in, but everything is still in place," he noted with relief.

"I wonder why the alarm didn't go on. We should check our security system," said Lucrecia as all three went downstairs into the kitchen.

Robert nodded, frowning. "Yes, definitely."

Lucrecia made tea while they waited for the police.

"But this has never happened before! I've only seen such things in movies," said Amelia, appalled.

"Are you all right, kid?" Robert gently hugged her by the shoulders.

"Yes... It seems like I scared the robber and he didn't have time to steal anything," she replied, pressing her head against her dad's shoulder.

"Yes, indeed. I admire your reaction, carinho. My girl is so brave!"

"Thank you, Dad. Have I done everything right?"

"Of course, my little kitten! I am so sorry you had to deal with this. I should have taken better precautions."

"Don't blame yourself, carinho," objected Lucrecia. "We thought we were safe here. It's the calmest neighborhood in the whole of São Paulo, so it was hard to expect anything like this... What do you think they might want? It's a bit too daring for ordinary burglars. Do you think it has something to do with your campaign?" she asked anxiously.

Robert sat at the table and put his hands on his lowered head.

"I have one rather unpleasant thought about it. There was only one potentially valuable item in my safe, and only a few people who knew about it. But it seems so surrealistic that I can hardly believe it... I will need to check all the facts before making suggestions. I'm not going to share these guesses with the police for now, as it could have serious consequences, but I definitely will take measures."

Overwhelmed and intrigued, Amelia switched her gaze from Father to Mother, who looked worried.

"I'll get in touch with the agency right away in the morning and make arrangements for a more decent security system, for both of our homes, here and in Lindageral. And I believe that hiring security guards will not be excessive after such a wake-up call."

"Agreed," nodded Lucrecia. "We knew what we signed up for, entering the deputy race."

"I wish you two were out of all this," said Robert guiltily.

Lucrecia put her hands on his shoulders.

"Everything will be all right. Always staying out of trouble is not the best way to live our lives. Our country needs changes, it needs wise people, and you are the one who can make these changes. We will be thoughtful and careful, and may Our Lady help us."

"You are right." Robert turned his head to kiss her hand. "I can't give up when I have two such brave women at my side."

"And anyway, Amelia will graduate in less than a month, and we will be off to the shores of England, to rock them with some Brazilian vibes, right, daughter?" Lucrecia winked at her. "Unless you change your plans again."

"No, I think I've made up my mind, for sure," said

Amelia, "I want to take that art course in London."

"Sounds great. So while Amelia and I are in England, you can get some rest from us and concentrate on your campaign."

CHAPTER TWO

"I LIKE THIS PLACE. IT'S SO PEACEFUL," Robert told his friend, Diego Campras, the Lindageral chief of police, as they sat with mugs of beer on his patio in the shadows of fig trees.

The late spring heat had subsided at dusk, and crickets were chirping around them.

"Yeah, definitely not like São Paulo," agreed Diego, "But believe me, a lot of things are happening here to keep us busy."

He took a sip of beer and looked at his friend questioningly.

"So, you think one of your companions is involved in your house break-in?"

Robert winced. "I hate to think about it. But the reality we need to face is that the only potentially valuable things in my home office were the technical schemes for the invention I discussed with them just before that. And they could easily figure out that I would take these papers elsewhere the next day."

"That would be a reckless move."

"No doubt. But the thing is that I wouldn't be able to prove anything in case they got the drawings and sold them somewhere else or made any other use of them. The design is not patented yet, and they could just modify it slightly and claim it was their own."

"Holy smokes, that's bad!" Diego scowled, setting his thick black mustache in motion. "You should be more careful, mate."

"I thought those people were trustworthy. I knew them for a while. It looks like I can't trust my judgment."

"Trust me. You never know what kind of gears are turning in people's heads and when they will go haywire. But you still have some good friends you can rely on."

He raised his glass, and Robert mirrored his move.

"Yes. Thank you."

"I will give you contacts from that security company. What else can I do for you? Do you want me to look through any information we have on those guys?"

"I don't think they would have any criminal records..."

"You should take a deeper look. Check their connections, family members, staff... Maybe it would make sense to hire a private investigator."

"I don't want to involve any outsiders in this. To be honest, I shouldn't have shared it even with you. I'm at the height of my election campaign now and don't have much time, but I'm trying to use my connections to get through the patenting process as fast as possible. Until then, it's a risky game," said Robert.

"Don't worry on my account. I assure you that your secrets are safe with me."

"Yes... Safety is what concerns me most about all the activities I'm involved in lately." Robert sighed heavily. "I wish my wife and daughter were far away from here and safe. I can't wait till Amelia's school is over. She wasn't happy to move here from São Paulo, but I believe it's much safer for her, for all of us here, in a small town, where everybody knows each other."

"It sure is. Don't worry. Nothing will happen on my watch," Bruno reassured him. "By the way, did you know that my son Marcelu is your daughter's classmate?"

"No way! That's awesome. No, I didn't know," said Robert with a smile.

"I realized it just now myself. I heard him talking about some Amelia, but it didn't ring any bells till you said her name. It seems he's quite impressed with your girl." Diego smirked. "We've heard a lot about her since the first day she came to his school. Marcelu says she's nothing like the other girls he's met. She's very smart and straightforward, in a good way. And that for the first time, he can speak to someone without playing dumb and not be afraid to be called a nerd."

"Well, it's music to a father's heart to hear such words about my daughter," admitted Robert with a wide grin. "But I guess she kind of has to stand out among local

Lindageral girls. After all, we didn't pay for all her private tutors and trips to Europe for no reason. Don't want to sound arrogant, but..."

"No need to explain, mate. I know that feeling of father's pride."

Robert nodded. "When she was born, I was so worried about if I could protect her from all the wrong that could be done to her and, at the same time, if she would become spoiled if we were overprotective. But it looks like we did well."

"I'm sure she's gonna be fine. And I will ask my son to look after her. If fact, I'm guessing I don't even need to ask him about it."

"I absolutely forgot that you had a son of the same age as my daughter," confessed Robert. He sipped his beer. "Our families should have spent more time together."

"Yes, definitely. I haven't seen you for four years. It's not something you could call frequent communication."

Robert looked puzzled. "It can't be four years... Oh, yeah. I guess you're right."

"I'm glad you decided to return to your homestead. Lindageral will be much better with you."

"I'll do as much as I can for it."

Diego nodded. "We need more authorities here. It's getting more and more hectic here lately."

"What do you mean?" Robert frowned.

"Remember, we had a High-Five supermarket on Figueira Street? Right, you don't remember. So, about half a year ago, some scoundrels broke in, took valuable items, and smashed what they couldn't take. The store shut down soon after."

"I think I know the owner of the High-Five chain. I met him several times at get-togethers."

"What's interesting... the same happened with their store in Brasopolis and in Aparecida."

"That can't be a coincidence." Robert nodded. "Looks like their competitors are trying to push them out of business."

"That's what I thought. If so, there is not much we can do. Those guys do smooth work. But the thing is they don't have any competitors here who could possibly do it. We have several local groceries and hardware stores, but..." Diego raised his hands. "I know them all and walk the same streets with them. I can't imagine anyone hiring a gang of mobsters to tear down their competitor's store."

"Well, if there are other big chain stores opening in these places any soon, we will have a clue."

"Yes, but I haven't heard of any so far."

"I guess there could be other reasons, like settling personal scores. You know how far people might go for that."

***

Amelia noticed something was up as soon as she entered the classroom. Her classmates were heatedly discussed something in hushed voices, looking excited and disturbed at the same time. As soon as Charlotta saw her, she parted from the other girls and sat at her desk like she couldn't wait to have a word with her.

Her parents had been in a constant state of anxious awareness during the past couple of weeks, busy updating their home security system, and she got an odd sense of synchronicity seeing her whole class so overwhelmed, like the whole world suddenly decided to go haywire.

"Hey, Charlotta. Good morning?" Amelia asked rather than claimed, taking a seat next to her friend.

"Have you heard what happened last night?" asked Charlotta in a muffled voice.

"No, what?"

"Do you know Marinio Risso, the owner of a grocery store? His daughter Elvina works as a cashier, a short girl with long black hair—remember her?"

"Yes, sure. And what about them?"

"Senhor Risso was found dead on the side of the road to Roseira, covered in stab wounds like a sieve!"

"Oh no, that's terrible!" gasped Amelia.

"It is! The police are looking for Elvina's boyfriend—they didn't get along well—and he was already in prison for beating a man half to death. And Elvina says that they fought badly the day before."

"Ugh... I hope they catch him soon. Having a madman hanging around the town isn't fun."

"Yes, absolutely! My mom said I shouldn't go out anywhere after dark now."

"I guess Elvina is the one in the most danger. He might come after her, especially if he hears that she sicced the police on him."

"Well noted, Amelia," said someone behind her.

She turned and saw Marselu, who'd just sat at the desk next to them. "I suggest we go to her and ask if we can help somehow."

His intrusiveness made Amelia wince, but this wasn't the right moment to get into an argument with him.

"I guess we could do it," she agreed, peering at him.

"Poor Elvina. Her mom died two years ago of cancer, and now she's completely alone! And she's just nineteen." Charlotta sighed. She looked at Marcelu then back at Amelia. "You wanna check up on her today, guys?"

"Sure. Let's go after school," suggested Marcelu. "I have soccer practice, but I can skip it."

"Are you sure it would be appropriate to disturb her? She might not have gotten over what happened yet," said Amelia doubtfully.

"Well, we could just ask if she needs anything, and if she doesn't feel like talking, we'll go," Marcelu reassured her.

"All right. I'll let my mom know. She picks me up after school, and she could give us a ride."

As Amelia had expected, Lucrecia appreciated their initiative and eagerly agreed to take Amelia and her friends to Elvina's place. A typical Lindageral house with white walls, terracotta roof tiles, and red window frames met them with an open door, covered with merely a mosquito net. They heard the indistinct sound of women's voices inside.

"Hello, is anybody there?" called Lucrecia.

A plump, round-faced woman with black hair done in a bun appeared in the doorway.

"Oh, Senhora Lucrecia! Hello and welcome! My name is Rosanna. I live next door. Come in. I was already leaving." The lady gracefully moved her voluptuous figure out of the doorway and let the visitors in.

Two younger women were sitting at the round dining table with two big trays of pastries. One of them stood up as they entered and anxiously stared at them with a pair of big brown eyes, puffed from crying.

"Hi, Elvina. We just wanted to say we are very sorry about what happened to your dear father," started Charlotta, who was on the closest terms with the girl.

"Thank you," Elvina said and hugged her.

"We also wanted to know if we can help with anything," said Lucrecia in her delicate, ladylike tone. "I guess you already know Amelia and Marcelu, and I am Amelia's mom. My name is Lucrecia."

"Yes, I sure do know you, Senhora del Atore! Thank you. You are very kind. Please come in and have a seat. I'll make you tea."

"Get some rest, Elvina. I'll take care of it," said the other guest, a slightly built woman with a blond pageboy haircut, dressed in a formal white blouse and gray skirt. She headed toward the kitchen cabinet to get mugs

"Thanks, Camilla." Elvina, who looked drained, gladly obeyed her.

"By the way, I'm Camilla Soares," said the blond girl. "I did accounting for Senhor Marinio, and I also came to assure Elvina that I would be happy to help her get into all the paperwork for their business... Her business now," she corrected herself.

"Yes, Father tried to keep me updated, but all these spreadsheets are still a puzzle for me..." Elvina sobbed as she spoke. "Camilla was so nice to offer me help. And Rosanna brought all this baking. Thank you all, ladies. I don't know what I would do without you."

"Don't worry, my dear. You are not alone." Lucrecia gently stroked the girl's shoulder. "I also would be happy to offer you free legal help with your inheritance and any other issues that may occur. I won't be able to deal with it myself as I am busy with other obligations, but I will find you a lawyer and cover all expenses."

"Thank you, Senhora. You are too kind!" Elvina burst into tears again.

"It's the least we can do for you. Our family is one of the keystones of our local community, and it's our responsibility to care about its members in need. With a little help, you will be able to continue your father's business, to the benefit of us all."

While they all kept silent for a while to let Elvina compose herself, Amelia looked at her mom with awe. She and her friends would certainly have felt awkward without her mom stepping forward and dealing with the drama with confidence and experience.

"Now, if you don't mind me asking, what's going on with your boyfriend? I heard that he tends to be... um... rather short-tempered," said Lucrecia.

Marcelu and Charlotta exchanged disturbed looks

with Amelia.

"Yes, he does... Luis and my father couldn't stand each other. That day, they had a terrible fight at the store, and Father kicked him out. I guess Luis asked him for money again. But I don't believe he could kill him. He's emotional and has his flaws, but he's not some psycho! Policemen just asked me if my father had any conflicts with anyone, and I told them about it. I probably shouldn't have. He had a term in prison already, and for sure, they will hang this on him." Elvina looked into the void with her big brown watery eyes.

"All right, let's leave it to the police to figure out if it was him or not," suggested Lucrecia. "Let's think about you first. Do you think Luis might get mad because he's a suspect and take it out on you?"

Elvina blinked in surprise several times.

"I'll take a look at your garden, if you don't mind, Elvina," Marcelu said and headed out through a back door.

"I don't think he would..." Elvina murmured.

"Has he ever hurt you before?" asked Lucrecia. "I know it's a weird question, and you don't have to answer, or we can talk later, one on one."

"No, not really... He can be a bit rough, can push me sometimes or slap when he gets mad or when he's drunk, but nothing serious. He never hit me for real," Elvina said reluctantly.

"I see." Lucrecia sighed. "Considering his previous criminal records, he should know better. He would be in real trouble."

Elvina nodded.

"You're right. I'm worried about him, Senhora Lucrecia. He's not a bad guy. He's strong, resolute... a master of his life. I don't know if I can cope with the business now without his help..."

"Don't worry. You won't be alone in any case. We will help you to figure things out," Lucrecia reassured her.

"For sure, Elvina," echoed Camilla. "I will go into all the accounting details with you, and you will catch up very quickly, I promise."

"Would you like to stay in our house for a couple days, until everything settles down?" suggested Lucrecia. "It's not good for you to be left alone now. We have a lot of free rooms, and Amelia would also be happy to have company. Right, daughter?"

"Sure," Amelia nodded.

"Oh, don't worry about me. I will be perfectly fine here," objected Elvina.

"Would you miss a chance to live in a nineteenth-century manor with original antique furniture? I remember how impressed I was when my husband first brought me there. It was like I traveled back in time. Only our house has modern air conditioning and cable television."

"Oh, I wish I could see it too," said Charlotta with awe.

Elvina smiled timidly. "All right. If you are sure that I will not disturb you..."

CHAPTER THREE

THE REST OF THE WEEK PASSED without significant news for residents of Lindageral, besides Luis Sanches, Elvina's fiancé, being arrested, much to the relief of everyone in town—including Elvina and her friends, though she felt guilty about acknowledging this.

The last week of school had come for Amelia's class. Almost all of them had already passed the national exam back in November, except for a few people who decided not to take it this year, so the atmosphere was laid-back and lax.

Nobody seemed to care much about studying, including teachers, who shared their own school memories and funny stories that had happened to them or gave them pep talks on starting their new lives. Some of the students already felt nostalgic about the years spent inside the school walls, while others just were bored and couldn't wait to be dismissed.

On Thursday, Marcelu approached Amelia during lunch break when she was alone in the classroom, writing in her notebook the list of books their teacher recommended for reading.

"Are you not going to eat today?" he asked.

"I am, in a few seconds. What do you want?"

"Nothing special... Actually"—he sat on the corner of her table—"I was going to go to the Alves farm and get a horse to ride. I was wondering if you would like to join me."

"They have horses for rent?" Amelia finally lifted her gaze from the notebook to look at him.

"Yes, and as Pedro Alves is my mom's cousin, he doesn't charge me and my friends any money."

"I don't really know..." said Amelia with visible hesitation. After noticing a self-satisfied smirk appearing on Marcelu's face, she added in a cold tone, "This is just another prank, isn't it?"

"I swear to you it isn't—Our Lady is my witness," said Marcelu, placing a palm above his heart. "I know you are still angry about that stupid joke, but I want to make amends with you. And I have something to say that you might want to know, Amelia."

"Like what?"

"I want to be sure there are no eavesdroppers around before talking about it. Something strange is going on lately, and it has something to do with your family."

His muffled whisper almost made Amelia shudder. She looked at him with disbelief, trying to guess whether he really knew something or had just hit the nail on the head by chance.

"Oh, right. Your dad is the police chief," she said, remembering, "and you probably heard from him that somebody attempted a robbery at our São Paulo house. My dad mentioned that he'd informed him and that we are expecting other attempts. As you probably know, my dad is a candidate for the Chamber of Deputies, and he is always in the crosshairs of his not-so-decent opponents, who might use all kinds of dirty tricks—you know how politics are done in our country—so I guess saying that something weird is going on around our family is an obvious shot in the dark…"

Amelia stopped to take a breath, and Marcelu, who'd patiently listened to her tirade, used the pause to say, "Yes, my dad is the chief, but you can be sure he doesn't discuss his work at the dinner table. But I have my eyes, and I observe what's going on in the town. Last night, I was riding my bike after dark and noticed something unusual."

"Then why don't you tell your policeman dad?"

"It wasn't illegal, just unusual. I mentioned it to him this morning, but there's nothing requiring police involvement."

Amelia kept staring at him with her scrutinizing gaze.

"Do you really think that I would take you out to do something bad to you? Do I look like some psychopath?

I'm your friend and a nice person."

"I guess that's what most psychopaths look like," retorted Amelia. "I'm not so simple-minded as to be impressed by your cheesy face."

"Cheesy face? Glad to know that you find me pretty," chuckled Marcelu, brushing a strand of his slightly wavy dark hair backward with his long fingers. Indeed, he was almost annoyingly pretty, with his deep-blue eyes framed with long black lashes; plump, curved lips; and milky-white skin, impervious to a suntan. Tall and slender, almost bony, he could be a model for deodorant advertising or an actor in some soapy teen sitcom.

"So, you didn't answer anything. Do you like horses?" continued Marcelu.

"Yes, I do."

"That's good. For some reason, I was sure you would like horse riding. Don't know why—perhaps because you look like a brave warrior princess, and a horse would be something very becoming." Marcelu gave her his most charming smile, which made her smile unwillingly as well.

"Ha! Boys and their fantasies!" She snorted. "All right, I guess I could do it, unless my mom has other plans for me."

Amelia decided not to tell Charlotta that she was going for a horse ride with Marcelu, not willing to look like a reneger in her friend's eyes after she'd stated she would never again keep company with him.

Lucrecia met them in the parking lot after the last bell rang and smiled benevolently at Marcelu.

"It's good that you're taking my daughter to clear her head. She spends too much time bent over the books and at the computer lately."

"Mom! You know very well that I was researching information about my school in London! That's what you told me to do," objected Amelia.

Her mother appeared to be sympathizing with Marcelu, which was strange and annoying.

The Alves farm was located on the northern end of Lindegeral, at a point where rows of whitewashed houses shaded by palm and acacia trees changed to green hills with pastures, orange groves, and coffee plantations surrounding the town. It was enclosed by a solid unpainted wooden fence with tall pillar-supported gates.

"Give me a call when you are done, and I'll come to pick you up," said Lucrecia when she dropped off Amelia and Marcelu. "Have fun, but be cautious."

"Have you ever ridden horseback before?" asked Marcelu, as Pedro Alves's son Ricardu, a stocky, swarthy guy about their age, led them to the stables.

"Yes, many times. Some of our friends have country estates and keep horses."

"Oh, that's good. So you know how to do it, then," Marcelu resumed with a hint of disappointment.

"Yes, but I can ride only with a saddle. I have no idea how to mount a horse without it."

"Don't worry about that. We have saddled horses for you," Ricardu told her with a smile.

"I prepared two very nice girls for you today. The bay mare is called Faísca"—he pointed at the chestnut-brown horse—"and the grullo one is Neblina." A silver-skinned horse moved her ears at the sound of her name.

"Which one will you choose, Amelia?" asked Marcelu.

"Faísca," she answered, reaching out to pet the horse whose shiny brown skin charmed her. "Will you carry me for a ride today, cutie?"

They mounted the horses, and Ricardu took Faísca's reins and led her through the gates, with Marcelu following on Neblina.

While they trotted toward the meadows, Amelia enjoyed the vibration of hooves hitting the pressed dirt road. She felt slightly nervous, as it had been a while since the last time she'd sat on a horse's back, but Faísca seemed to be cooperative, and she quickly regained the heady feeling of merging into one with a horse.

As the road led them toward open space away from the town road where occasional cars, cyclists, or pedestrians could pop up on their way, they sped up to a gallop.

They passed along an alley running through the orange grove, endless rows of green ellipses of crowns heavily festooned with ripening fruits. Behind the fields was a small creek, wiggling its way through the green meadow.

"Let's stop here!" shouted Marcelu.

Amelia pulled on the reins slightly, and Faísca obediently stopped. They dismounted. Amelia ran her hand over Faísca's glossy skin, slightly moist with sweat, feeling the muscles of her neck and chest.

"They are awesome, aren't they?" said Marcelu, watching her petting the horse.

"Yes, they are! I wish we had horses, but my mom didn't want to get even a dog, with our busy and hectic lifestyle."

"We have a dog. Airedale terrier, big and fluffy. You could come and see her sometimes."

"Maybe... So, what was that important information you wanted to share with me? Or was it just an excuse?"

"Why are you so mistrustful?" lamented Marcelu, raising his hands and eyes to the sky in disappointment. "I'm getting to that point."

"Fire away, then!"

"So, as I said, a few days ago, I went for a late bicycle ride. I like to do it after sunset, when it's not hot and the streets are empty. I made a circle around the town, and when I was passing by your neighborhood, I noticed a group of people with TV cameras and lights. I recognized Leon Wargas, the reporter. Do you know him?"

"Wargas? I think I've heard this name but can't remember who he was."

"He's an independent journalist who has made his name by investigating the crimes of major politicians and businesspeople. He's a pain in the ass for all corrupt bosses. But now, he is sniffing around your family manor. I completely forgot to tell you with all these things happening. But yesterday, I saw your dad's ad on the TV, and it led me to wondering if Wargas is trying to dig up something on him."

"What? No, my father is the most decent man and

politician you could think of. He's never done anything that would potentially draw Leon Wargas's attention."

"Well, maybe your father's political opponents fed Wargas some fake incriminating evidence against him," suggested Marcelu, "and even if your father could prove it wrong afterward, there will be an impact on people's opinion. Leon Wargas has a reputation as an honest and incorruptible reporter."

Impressed, Amelia was silent for a minute. "I should tell my parents about it," she said next. "I'm sure they have nothing to hide. Maybe they would want to talk to Wargas and ask what he's up to."

"Don't get me wrong. I know that your parents are awesome people, and they have done a lot for Lindageral and our school, and they are loved and supported here—I especially appreciate that they funded the road repair. But there were some dark pages in your family history, which your father's opponents will use for sure."

"Yes, I'm aware that we are descendants of Portuguese colonists who made their fortune using slave labor on plantations. But now, we are on a completely different page. My family is supporting public schools and hospitals and has opened a shelter for women and children in São Paulo..."

"I'm not talking about your ancestors from the eighteenth century... There were members of your family less remote from you, like the infamous Amarillio del Atore, your grandfather, who got away with killing his own brother and wife, erasing his competitors by any means, and committing countless acts of kidnapping, rape, and mutilation."

Amelia frowned. "Is any of this proven fact, or is it just a spooky story?"

"He kept the police bosses in his pocket and never got charged with any crimes. But many people in São Paulo, Lindageral, and its outskirts hundreds of kilometers around could share such stories that happened to either them or someone from their family. My father himself has talked with his victims while he was on duty as a regular police officer, and he felt powerless. There was nothing he could do. Is this really news for you?" asked Marcelu disbelievingly, looking at the stunned expression on Amelia's face as they stood facing each other, holding the horses' reins.

"It's the first time I've heard about it. My grandfather was a creepy man, and he and my dad didn't get along and stayed distant, and I met him only a few times in my life before he died three years ago, but it never occurred to me that he could be some kind of maniac."

"A maniac possessing incredible power and authority and an extraordinary mind—it's a very dangerous kind."

"My parents never talked about him in my presence, but I heard from someone that they got into a serious fight with him because he didn't approve of my mom as his son's wife. Knowing my mom, I guess that's because she couldn't help sassing him, I guess. So right after they got married, they moved to Portugal, where I was born."

Marcelu nodded. "That was a wise decision,

considering what happened to your father's first wife."

"What do you mean?" Amelia frowned. "I knew that my dad was married before, and his first wife died in a terrible car accident less than one year after their wedding. Her body got burned to ashes. I didn't know until three years ago, when Mom and I organized things in the attic in our house and found the wedding pictures. They'd never mentioned it to me before, but I don't blame them. It's not something people discuss easily. I was fifteen at that time, and the story shocked me so much that I had nightmares afterward."

"Once again, I have no proof, but some people say that Amarillio had something to do with this. She was a very pretty and shy girl, and he started molesting her. The circumstances of her death were suspicious enough. She crashed her car on an empty road, and it exploded and burned to coals. But of course, police found nothing criminal in the accident."

"Oh my, that's really creepy," whispered Amelia. "I never liked him, but this... I can't even wrap my head around it."

"Yes, but I guess your father found a way to stop Amarillio somehow. At least, soon after Robert returned from Portugal with you and your mom, Amarillio stepped down as a chairman of the Campoverde, passing the reins over to his son, and became a shut-in."

"How do you know all that?" Amelia raised her eyebrows. "You were three years old at that time, as far as I know."

"Yes, but I heard it from my dad and other people.

I was always very curious and asked many questions." Marcelu smiled. "But returning to where we started, what brought Leon Wargas to your family land?"

"I guess you already have some smart theories," said Amelia derisively.

"Well, I just asked myself how I could possibly use the dark stain of being a son of a cruel mafioso to do serious damage to your father's reputation, if I were his opponent. And I realized one thing: the crimes of his father were never investigated. The voices of hundreds of broken lives crying for justice remained muted. If Robert del Atore is indeed that honorable man deemed to bring our country to a better future, why didn't he start with cleaning his family closet? He didn't have enough guts to get his own father sent to prison?"

"You said your father heard testimonies of several Amarillio's victims. Why didn't he pursue him to hold him accountable for what he'd done? He's a police chief, after all," Amelia said to parry his arguments.

"My father is not a politician, and he doesn't have opponents willing to drown him. And he's doing as much as he can. You don't always get to make amends for what happened in the past when you are busy trying to do what should be done right now... And I guess that also is the case with your father. I didn't mean to accuse him—I'm just trying to show how somebody could interpret things if they have this goal."

"That makes sense," agreed Amelia, stroking Faísca's neck. "Thank you for sharing this with me. I will talk with my parents, and I suppose they would like to have a word with you as well. You seem to be surprisingly knowledgeable.”

"I just see and observe, as Sherlock Holmes said." Marcelu smiled. "Probably because I read a lot of detective stories as a child. Or because my dad is a policeman, it's in my blood."

The sun had already started setting, painting the green grass with gold, and the red soil seemed to be burning in its beams. The air was filled with a humid smell from the creek.

"Should we head back?" suggested Marcelu, looking at her. "It will start getting dark pretty soon."

Amelia had gone silent, reflecting on what she just heard. "Sure."

"Sorry if it was too much for you to hear. I didn't mean to shock you."

"That's fine. It's good to be aware. And those are things I would never dare to ask my parents about."

Amelia was deep in her thoughts all the way back to the farm, reflecting on how little she actually knew about what was going on around her. How little she knew about life, her land, and her people. Of course, she was good at Brazilian history and could name all its leaders and tell what determined their politics, but she didn't know about what had been going on in the last two decades with the people she met every day on Lindageral's streets and in school, the grocery store, or the library. She also didn't know what impact her family had made on their lives.

She asked herself if she really needed to know. In just a few weeks, she would be thousands of kilometers away, in England, another part of the world, where it would be summer while it was winter here. And for the next four or more years, she would be breathing the fogs of England, eating English food, speaking English, and making new British friends. Who knew—maybe she would never return to Brazil, save for visiting her parents and friends once or twice a year.

Unless...

For her entire life, she'd lived in a small bubble of safety her parents created for her, surrounded by the likes of them—her parents' friends, well-off educated people and their children, her classmates from private schools she attended—the people who spoke multiple languages, traveled all around the world, and could compare the perks of Sydney's opera theatre against those of Vienna's.

The world felt welcoming and cozy, and everybody seemed to love her and her family, especially here in the small community of Lindageral, where everybody seemed to know her everywhere she went.

But now, exactly at the moment when she was about to open the door leading to adult life with its serious decisions, her trust in the world around her was cracking. First, somebody broke into their house, and her father was acting like he'd expected it. Then she heard the shocking revelation about her grandfather. The idea that her father might not be a good person was inconceivable to her, and she discarded it, but the dawning realization of how little she knew was quite sickening.

"What are you thinking about?" asked Marcelu after they returned the horses to the stable and sat on a bench in the Alves's yard, waiting for Amelia's mother to pick her up.

"Um... nothing in particular. By the way, I remember you mentioned that you are going to study in Santos?"

"Not quite. That was one of the backup options, but I already received confirmation from the University of São Paulo. I am enrolled in the criminology course, and I'm starting in February." Marcelu smiled with undisguised pride.

"Oh, good for you!"

"But you're going to England. That's much cooler!"

"Yes, I will take a short-term course in art first, just to see if it's something I want to do."

"That's good when you can try different things and drop out whenever you like," said Marcelu with a note of envy in his voice. "My parents saved money for my education for years, and they would kill me if I wasn't sure what I want to do. You are a lucky duck."

"Yes, I guess so," agreed Amelia, feeling slightly guilty.

"So, when are you heading to England?"

"My course starts in February, but my mom wants us to leave right away, in the next couple weeks, so that we can do a little bit of traveling and exploring and I can take English courses, just to feel more confident in my studies."

"I thought you already knew English better than Englishmen. I've seen you reading books in English without a dictionary."

"There is always room for an upgrade." She shrugged.

"So you are leaving very soon, then? That's sad. We just started getting to know each other better."

Amelia raised her eyebrows. "I don't know what's going on in your imagination, but I went for this ride with you only because you intrigued me with your story."

"I guess you're still angry at me because of that prank? I can explain. It wasn't my idea. Pablo wanted to do it, and I tried to stop him, but the guys started to mock me and make some stupid suggestions like... you know.

So I said that I'd do it myself, just to make them shut up."

"Sorry, what?" Amelia stared in utter disbelief. "You did it just to not look stupid in front of your friends? And you believe you were protecting my honor or something? That's some perverted reverse psychology."

"Well, sort of... And most importantly, I didn't want any conflicts with them, as they are an important source of information on what's going on in town. And there is definitely something unusual going on recently."

"Right. So, you are the neighborhood watch, then?"

"Kind of." Marcelu smiled. "So, will you forgive me?"

Amelia gave him an examining look. "I forgive you. As long as you don't play a fool again."

"I solemnly swear it was the first and the last time. Never again." Marcelu put his hand to his heart with exaggerated pathos. "I hope we can be friends again and enjoy the time we have left to spend together."

*****

Saturday was the big day all Lindageral's school graduates had waited for and talked about for the past couple months, their graduation party. It was especially exciting because the school board had hired the famous DJ Maretimo to play for them, with a little help from the del Atore family.

Amelia put on the sparkly blue-green-and-pink strapless dress she'd prepared for this occasion, completing the outfit with drop earrings with rhinestones, a necklace with a pendant, and metallic pink ballerina shoes that matched her dress, comfortable enough for her to spend a few hours on her feet and dance.

Lucrecia curled her daughter's long auburn hair with a curling iron and applied sophisticated makeup to her face with eyeliner and pink and gray shadows, making her hazel eyes look especially deep and bright.

"You're going to shine today, carinho!" she said with satisfaction, contemplating the result.

Showtime was at five, but Amelia and her mother volunteered to help with decorating the patio and schoolyard, so they arrived at the school by three.

When they arrived, a group of teachers and parents already had preparations well underway, music equipment was installed at the patio, and somebody was wrapping an LED garland around its pillars. The day was hot and the air dense and filled with scents of sun-warmed flowers in baskets, surrounding the patio. The cheerful sound of samba splattered around from the speakers installed on the stage.

"Oh, I left the Congratulations banner in the car," Lucrecia suddenly remembered. She had her hands full of party supplies. "Amelia, dear, could you please go and fetch it for me? It should be somewhere on the backseat." She passed what she was holding to a woman who came to greet them and handed the keys to her daughter.

Amelia went to the parking lot and got the banner they'd ordered from her mother's Audi A5. It read Godspeed, Kids of Lindageral. When she was closing the car door, she noticed the hunched figure of an elderly woman standing at some distance. Something strange about her caught Amelia's eyes and made her take a closer look. While the temperature was more than thirty degrees Celsius in the shade, the woman was wearing a long-sleeve jacket, and her head was wrapped in a dense shawl of the same shabby gray tone as her dress and jacket.

"Hello," Amelia said as their eyes met.

"You look so splendid today," the woman said, examining the girl with the fixed gaze of her faded blue eyes, which gave her emaciated and blemished face a wild, insane look.

"Oh, thank you..."

"It is such a great day for you, Amelia. You will remember it for a long time."

"Do you know me?" asked Amelia with some confusion. "Sorry. I can't remember if we've met before."

"My name is Dolores, and I know a lot about you," she said in a hollow tone. "I can see things others cannot see." She suddenly stepped forward and took one of Amelia's hands between hers, which were weirdly cold. "Beware, Amelia, something very evil is approaching you. Everywhere you go, do watch your back."

She was stunned for a moment. "What do you mean?" she asked hesitantly.

Dolores just shook her head.

Amelia realized the woman wasn't as old as she'd first thought. She seemed more like she was worn out by some disease devouring her from the inside. Amelia didn't know much about mental disorders, but that looked like it was the case.

"All right, Senhora Dolores. I will be careful. Thank you. Is there anything I can do for you?"

"Take care of yourself," said the woman. She gave Amelia another long stern look then turned away. "Go home before it's dark tonight!" the woman called out as she walked away with an unsteady gait.

The strange woman's vicious words gave Amelia a chill down her spine in the middle of the hot December day.

Why did the whole world suddenly decide to go crazy?

She returned to the schoolyard, where her mother was already bustling around with other volunteers.

"Here it is." Amelia handed the banner to her. "Sorry for the delay. There was some strange lady who started talking to me..."

“A strange lady? What did she want?”

“Just some nutter. She muttered some nonsense.” Amelia didn’t want her mom to get even more stressed out.

“Oh… All right, could you please help Senhora Libia? She’s filling balloons with helium.”

After two hours passed, the schoolyard was shining with the warm lights of the LED garlands, and the patio’s roof was looking like it was ready to take off into the air with all the balloons attached to it. Festively dressed and cheerful newly minted graduates started to arrive, filling the air with chatter and laughter.

Somebody touched Amelia’s elbow. She turned her head and was not surprised to see Marcelu, wearing a short-sleeved blue shirt neatly tucked into black trousers, his hair styled with wax.

“Hey, there. You are all glowing tonight!” he greeted Amelia.

“Thanks.” She smiled at him. “It’s all Charlotta. She covered my face with glitter.”

Amelia nodded at her friend, who also had sparkles over her cheeks. Charlotta’s curly hair looked even more voluminous that day, and she was dressed in a long silky black dress with golden stripes and a slit on its right.

“You both are gorgeous tonight!” said Marcelu.

“You are also not so bad,” noted Amelia benevolently.

The celebrated DJ pumped up his stereo system, shaking the space with techno rhythms, and they started to dance.

It wasn't the fanciest party Amelia had been to, but the atmosphere of cheer and unity made it special and enveloped her in its softness like black velvet.

"Such a beautiful night," Marcelu noted to the girls as they were drinking champagne out of plastic glasses while the DJ paused to tune his equipment. "We should leave town to see the stars."

"What? Right now?" Charlotta chuckled.

"Sure. Let's make this night memorable. I know a perfect secluded spot on the river with a smooth sandy bank. It will be a perfect time, when it's so quiet, and you can see the reflections of the moon and stars on the expanse of the water."

"Wow, you're a romantic. I would never have guessed," scoffed Amelia.

"Sometimes. Only on special occasions, like today," he agreed with a wink. "So what, would you like to give it a try? It's just a ten-minute drive away. I have a car and can drive us there. It's a full moon tonight, and you have my word it's worth seeing."

"What you think, Charlotta? Do you want to go?" asked Amelia.

"Are you sure you need a third someone there?" She smiled.

"Of course! What is that you're implying? If you aren't going, neither am I."

"All right then. Let's go together," agreed Charlotta. "There's no chance I'm letting you miss the fun."

"So, you agree, then?" asked Marcelu.

"Only if it will not take more than an hour. My

mom went home, but she will be back for me at midnight. She wouldn't be happy with it, but it should be fine if she doesn't notice my absence."

"Oh, somebody is being a very naughty girl tonight." Charlotta smiled.

"All right, let's sneak out of here." Marcelu nudged them. "I parked the car down the street."

They made their way through the crowd and out of the schoolyard and headed towards a narrow, hardly illuminated side street.

"Amelia!" a man called.

She stopped. A chunky man in a black T-shirt got out of a van parked on a corner.

"Your mom asked me to drive you home," he said. "She is feeling bad."

"Do I know you?"

"I'm your neighbour. You don't remember me?"

"No..."

While she was wondering what to do, somebody grabbed her from behind and pulled her toward the van. Having not even realized what was going on, she kicked the man in front of her in his knee then squatted down to free herself from the other's grip and started to run.

Marcelu and Charlotta, who'd proceeded forward without noticing that she'd stopped to talk to someone, looked back as they heard the noise. Charlotta screamed. Marcelu ran towards Amelia.

The duo of assailants jumped back in the van, and it quickly took off, speeding up along the street.

"Damn... Are you all right?" asked Marcelu.

Amelia didn't answer, as she was busy adjusting her dress, which got twisted around her and pulled up, embarrassingly revealing her underwear.

"This cocktail dress definitely isn't designed for a fight," she muttered.

"Oh my God, what was that?" screeched Charlotta. "Were these jerks just sitting here waiting for girls coming from the party?"

"It looks like they were waiting for me specifically. He called me by name and started saying about something about my mom asking him to give me a ride home, and he managed to get me confused like a three-year-old kid," Amelia blurted out, indignant and hitting herself in the forehead with a palm.

Marcelu and Charlotta looked at her with concern.

"That stinks really bad," said Marcelu. "We should call the police. Or better, go to their office. I'll call my dad and ask what to do."

"Right," conceded Amelia. "Thank you,"

What was concerning her the most at the moment was the image of her mother in her head, telling her, *"Have you lost your mind? What you were even thinking? I thought you were smarter than that."*

"Dad told me to take you both to the police office, and he will be there in five minutes," said Marcelu after a short phone call. "Charlotta, would you mind being a witness? I'm so sorry to get you involved in this. I hope it won't take them long to take a statement from you, and then I can drive you home."

"All right," said the girl.

"I should also call my mom," said Amelia. "Oh no, my clutch! I must have dropped it!" she suddenly realized.

Marcelu frowned. "Are you sure you had it with you?"

"Sure, I had my phone and wallet in it!"

They returned to the place of the incident, but the clutch wasn't there.

"Sorry about that," said Marcelu. "Was your phone expensive?"

"Not really. I'd had it for three years already. And that's not what I'm worried about. If those guys took my phone, they might steal all my personal data. But never mind—I didn't have anything compromising in it anyway."

"Did you guys notice any numbers on the license plate?" asked Charlotta.

"I tried, but all I could read is that it was a São Paulo number with the letters *BFA*, but I could read just the first number, seven. The rest was covered with dirt—on purpose, I guess," said Marcelu.

"Clever bastards," muttered Amelia. "It's good that you paid attention. I absolutely forgot to take a look."

"That's fine. You were stressed out. Don't be so hard on yourself. Actually, I also noticed that the left taillight on the van wasn't working. And there was a distinct bump on the back. The make is Volkswagen, Transporter or LT. I'm not an expert, but our neighbors have a similar one, just blue. It's not much of a clue, but at least it's something."

When they arrived at the police office, Marcelu's

father, Police Chief Captain Diego Campras, was already waiting for them at the entrance.

"Hey, folks. It seems like your night did not go the way you planned?" He commented, giving them a quick questioning look. "But don't stress too much. It's not a proper graduation party if you don't end up in a police office after it. At least you aren't under arrest. For now."

The girls chuckled.

Marcelu rolled his eyes, muttering "Dad!"

"You are Amelia, right?" asked Captain Campras, looking at her.

She nodded.

"Are you all right? Any injuries? Do you need a doctor?"

"No, I'm fine. Some people attacked me near the school. It seems like they tried to kidnap me, but I was able to escape."

"Actually, that was quite impressive. Do you have a black belt in martial arts or something?" asked Marcelu.

"No, only a brown with a black stripe. Brazilian jiujitsu. I just used the simplest technique to get out of their grip. Didn't have to fight with them." Then she realized something. "I forgot to call my mom! Can I use somebody's phone?"

"I already reached your mom. She should be here soon," Diego reassured her.

"Oh, thank you," said Amelia, relieved that she didn't have to deal with her mom's first reaction.

"Let's go to my office, and I will hear your detailed story. Our duty officer, Gabriel Andrade, will talk to your friends in the meanwhile."

A tall, dark-skinned man standing behind the chief nodded to them.

The chief's office was not a big room, with a computer desk, a big monitor on a wall, a barred window covered by louvers, beige linoleum on the floor, and four chairs for visitors, one of which was placed near his desk. As she sat on a chair, Amelia noticed a framed black-and-white portrait of Juscelino Kubitschek in morning dress with a white bow tie and the Order of the British Empire.

"I see you're a fan of JK. I'm in your league as well," said Amelia, nodding at the portrait. "He is the greatest president our country has ever had."

"Yes, indeed. Our country needs more people like him. Who knows? Maybe your dad will also become president one day. I'm sure he could be just as brilliant as JK," suggested the captain. "You can call me Diego. Did you know we were good friends with Robert?"

Amelia shook her head.

"Yes, although we don't get to see each other often since we've become adults. And now it seems like you and my son have become friends. Isn't it amazing how things turn out sometimes?"

"Yes, it is." She was feeling annoyed by this sentimental small talk, even though she realized the captain probably just wanted to relieve her stress.

"I'll make you a coffee. You need a hot, sweet drink." Diego turned on an electric kettle on a small stand near the wall and gave Amelia an examining look. "I must admit you have enviable composure."

"I guess I still haven't realized what happened," admitted Amelia. "It was all so fast..."

"That's fine." Diego stirred instant coffee and sugar into a mug and handed it to her. "Here, have a drink. It should help you to get your thoughts together."

Amelia mechanically took a few sips before realizing the coffee was disgusting.

"Could you please tell me the sequence of things that happened, with as many details as possible?"

She spoke, while the captain took notes on his computer. When they finished, Diego left of the room and returned with Lucrecia.

"Mom! I'm so sorry," Amelia said preventively. "I know I shouldn't have gone anywhere without discussing it with you..."

"We will talk about this later. Are you all right?" asked Lucrecia, who looked tense but maintained her self-control.

"Yes, I'm fine. Don't worry."

"It seems like my son is a bad influence on her, Lucrecia. I will have a serious conversation with him," said Diego.

Amelia wasn't sure whether he was serious or just trying to butter up her mother—his mustachioed face always had that sly expression.

"You definitely should do that," said Lucrecia coldly. "Let's go, Amelia."

She followed her mother out of the office. Charlotta and Marcelu were sitting on a bench in the lobby and looked at them questioningly. Lucrecia walked past without stopping.

"Thanks for helping, guys. Talk later." That was all she had time to say, trying not to fall behind.

She felt nauseated from exhaustion and the captain's bad coffee. As they went outside, Amelia shivered either because of the cool night air or because the shock of the recent incident finally caught up to her.

Lucrecia took off her blazer and put it on her. "So, may I hear what exactly has happened?" she asked in a neutral tone.

Amelia repeated the story she just told the police chief. Mother listened without interruptions.

"So, these people were waiting for you in a van at the exact same time when Marcelu asked you to go for a drive? That raises some questions," she pointed out when Amelia finished.

"What do you mean?" gasped Amelia. "Do you think he may be involved in this?"

"That looks very probable to me."

"But... but he is the son of the police chief. Why would he do it?"

"Bah! That doesn't change anything," spat Lucrecia, "except the fact that it would be easier for him to get away with anything."

"I don't think so... He looked shocked, not like he'd expected something like this."

"Oh, Amelia, you are so naive!" Lucrecia sighed.

"But why would he do something like this?"

"I don't know. We should first ask what the purpose of the kidnappers was. And there are a few obvious reasons, unfortunately."

As they arrived home, Lucrecia opened the tall metal gate leading to their house driveway with a remote control, unlocked the newly installed security system, and parked the car in the garage.

"Have a seat, please," she told Amelia as they entered the living room.

Amelia obediently sat on one of the beige couches. Mother sat on the other end, facing her.

"Listen to me, please. This all is very serious. I hope you understand it now."

Amelia nodded.

"I want you to cut all contact with Marcelu Campras for now, until the situation clears up."

"All right. But I still don't think he has anything to do with it. After all, if he'd meant any harm to me, he could have done it when we were riding horses!"

"Yes. Now I realise that I shouldn't have let you go with him that time. But at least I was aware that you were with him then. And this kidnapping might have not been planned by then. Did you tell anyone at school where you were going this time?"

"No. Only Charlotta, but she was with us." Amelia looked at her mother doubtfully. "I really don't think that—"

"Believe me, I also hope that it was just a coincidence and Marcelu had nothing to do with that. I know he is a nice guy. It would be sad if he was a scoundrel." Lucrecia patted Amelia's shoulder and smiled with an all-knowing look on her face.

"Well, he is an idiot capable of many stupid jokes, but that would be too much for him. But I agree with you. I'm staying out of trouble till things clear up."

"That's a wise decision," said Lucrecia. "Well, it's very late. You need to get some rest. Don't worry about anything. It's all over. You are safe now."

"Yes, Mom," said Amelia, and they exchanged an embrace.

She took a shower and fell asleep as soon as her head reached her pillow.

CHAPTER FOUR

BRIGHT SUNLIGHT SQUEEZING UNDER heavy blinds had woken Amelia. She looked at the electronic clock on her nightstand—it showed half past ten in the morning already. She went downstairs in her pajamas to the rumble of her parents' voices as they discussed something in the living room.

"Here is my princess," Robert stepped forward to give her a hug as she entered.

"Good morning! Dad, you're back!"

"Just came. Sorry, my meeting with the governor finished very late yesterday. Dammit, I should have canceled it and gone to your party instead." He examined her from top to bottom with a concerned look. "Holy Mother, I am so sorry. Your mom just told me what happened." He ran out of breath, grasped Amelia in his arms again, and took a loud breath.

"I'm fine, Dad, seriously! Nothing really bad happened," Amelia assured him, afraid he would start to cry.

"I know you showed that scum you are too tough to deal with. That's my girl!"

"I mostly just used the easiest escape technique, and then they saw my friends and ran. I didn't get to fight for real," explained Amelia. "I wonder if I could if I had to, though"

Lucrecia sighed and shook her head. "If you want to prove that you're good at sparring, better get your black belt instead of getting into street fights."

"Sure, Mom. I'm not going to get in trouble just to prove something," Amelia told her.

"Glad to hear. I'll go make breakfast for my fresh grad!"

Amelia had just finished eating her scrambled eggs and toast with blueberry jam, and somebody rang the bell at the gates. Robert went to answer the intercom. It had a newly installed monitor, showing a video feed from the entrance.

"Who is that?" asked Lucrecia from the kitchen.

"It's the police," said Robert, approaching them. "They want to talk with Amelia."

"What, again? She already told them everything last night," grumbled Lucrecia.

While Robert went to open the door, Amelia quickly finished her orange juice and went to the living room, accompanied by her mother.

Two uniformed men appeared at their doorway.

One, a tall, scrawny man, introduced himself. "Inspector Renaldo Teixeira." With a grumpy expression, he showed his identification card. "This is my partner, Officer Silva." He pointed at the chubby black-skinned man, who also showed his ID. "Where can we talk to Senhorita Amelia?"

"Please come in," said Robert, waving them in.

Teixeira entered the living room and sat on a couch, while Silva kept standing near the door. Amelia and her parents sat on another couch across from them.

"We have your report about the attack on you last night," started Teixeira.

Amelia nodded.

"Did you lose any personal belongings during this incident?"

"Yes. I've lost a clutch with my cell phone and my wallet. I think it was mentioned in my report."

"What did it look like?"

"The clutch? It was black, with a metallic chain for a handle. The phone was Samsung, with an anime-design case on it. And a brown leather wallet. I had my library card and credit card with my name on it."

"We found your belongings," said Teixeira, looking at her without expression.

"Oh, great!" said Amelia. "How can I get it back?"

"I'm afraid we cannot give it back to you anytime soon. They are evidence, as they were found at a crime scene. Near a dead body."

"What?" gasped Lucrecia.

Amelia froze, looking at the inspector.

"A dead man's body was found this morning at the grove less than a kilometer away from your house."

All three of them looked at one another in utter shock.

"Do you know his identity?" asked Robert.

"We're currently working on it. Looks like he's not local." Teixeira opened a picture on his phone and showed it to Amelia. "Do you recognize this person?"

Amelia shuddered inwardly when she saw a distorted, dead face on the screen.

"I... I think I do," she murmured hesitantly. "It seems it is one of the men who attacked me. He was the one who talked to me and said he was our neighbor."

His wide eyebrows and straight hairline had imprinted in her memory. Seeing him dead after just a matter of hours was bizarre.

"How did he die?" asked Amelia.

"Stabbed in his heart. Died on the spot." Teixeira put the phone back in his pocket. "Where were you last night between one and five a.m.?" he asked Amelia.

"Home, sleeping. I came home soon after one a.m., and I woke up less than an hour ago."

"Can your parents confirm that?"

"Robert came home from São Paulo after nine today, but I was home with my daughter all this time," said Lucrecia.

"Are you sure that she stayed inside all this time?" asked Teixeira.

"Of course I am sure!" spat Lucrecia with

indignation. "May I ask, what is the reason for such questions? Do you suspect my daughter of something? Do you really think she would sneak out of home at night to hunt down a bandit who'd just attacked her?"

"It's just standard procedure, senhora. Keep calm, please," responded Teixeira, making notes in his notepad.

"But it's ridiculous! My poor girl was barely standing on her feet!"

"We have cameras surveilling the whole perimeter of the house," said Robert. "We can check the records."

"Excellent!" exclaimed Teixeira. "That makes everything easier. We can check it now, and later, I will send a technical expert to make a copy of the records. We also have to take fingerprints—your daughter's and yours and Senhora Lucrecia's, just in case."

"Very well," said Robert. "Act according to your procedure. I believe we should be worried about a murderer killing people near our house rather than this."

Teixeira took an electronic fingerprint scanner from his folder and got all three of them to press their fingers to it.

After they were done, Robert took both policemen to the computer room to check the records.

"What the hell," whispered Amelia heatedly after she was left alone with her mother in the living room.

"Well, when it rains, it pours," sighed Lucrecia. "Don't lose your cool. We will get through it. Very soon, you will be far from this mess, sketching the beautiful architecture of London and making new friends."

"Unless they arrest me."

"Don't panic. Nobody is going to arrest you. I'm sure the police will understand that you are just a victim in this chain of mishaps."

"It seems like this Teixeira doesn't like me."

"I believe it's just his regular demeanor. Just in case, we'll ask Diego Campras to take control. Be sure I'm going to use all of our resources, whatever it takes. You are starting your new adult life, and you deserve everything to go smoothly without having your plans destroyed by this bullshit," said Lucrecia firmly.

"Thank you, Mom."

Amelia pondered her Mother's words: *"Use all of our resourses."* This phrase brought up the involuntary memory of what Marcelu had said of her grandfather's atrocious crimes: *"He kept the police bosses in his pocket and never got charged with any crimes."* Then she heard another voice sneering in her head: *"But when good people do it, it's a completely different thing, isn't it?"*

Robert returned with Inspectors Teixeira and Silva.

"We watched the records in fast forward, and it confirmed what you said. Nobody exited the house after one fifteen a.m." announced Teixeira.

Amelia and Lucrecia nodded at what was obvious to them.

"I am sorry this all happened to your family," said Teixeira, "but we will do the best we can to figure things out. We will keep you updated."

After the officers left, Robert sat on a couch in exhaustion and pressed his hands to his face for a moment.

"Don't worry, Dad. I didn't kill that guy. They can't hang it on me. In case they do, I always can escape to Argentina," Amelia tried to joke. She hated seeing her dad in such a perplexed state—it made her feel utterly guilty and awkward. "I'm not sure if the British Police have a treaty with ours about extradition of people suspected in crimes. Maybe Britain could also be a good place to hide. If not, going to Matu Grossu to herd cows could also be an option. Or I could go to Roraima and live with an indigenous tribe. I always wondered what it's like. What do you think? Would I be able to blend in?"

"For Christ's sake, Amelia, stop this stream of nonsense," said Lucrecia with irritation.

"Sorry, Mom. It's just stress. What do you want me to do?"

"Let's just keep calm and proceed with our initial plan. Leaving the country as soon as possible would be the best and safest option, as long as we are not restricted by any orders. Of course, all this fuss with the police will settle down eventually, but precious time could be lost if they start hindering us, and I don't want that for you."

"Neither do I," agreed Amelia.

"I will check tickets to London right now and book the first available spot."

"Hmm. But how would that look? A daughter of a candidate to the Parliament leaves the country in a hurry, under cover of darkness, while the police consider her a main suspect in a murder case." Amelia ran her index finger through the air as if reading the words. "Imagine the headlines in the media."

"You think the line 'Daughter of a candidate for Parliament is arrested on suspicion of homicide' would sound much better?" scoffed Lucrecia. "The sad truth about the world is that people tend to sympathize with the strong one, not the innocent one. They believe in higher justice, in laws of karma, in 'no smoke without fire,' and whatever other balderdash they can come up with to deal with the bare truth that good and bad luck are simply a roll of the dice and there's no greater meaning behind it... So if you let yourself get arrested, nobody would think that you did it because you were too conscientious to use your resources for evading arrest." She took a deep breath and continued, "You will have a professional representative protecting your good name while you will study and mind your own business."

"Your mom is right, Amelia," interjected Robert. "It's better not to test fate."

"All right," Amelia said. "If you believe it's the best option..."

"Very good. Now, I suggest you write down a list of what you need to pack, and I will deal with the rest. Don't forget it's winter in England, so you will need some warm clothes and a jacket, but don't pack a lot of stuff, just what's basic and essential for a couple days. We can buy everything else you may need in London."

Amelia went upstairs to her room and opened her closet and drawers, trying to get an idea of what she might need to pack. She used to travel a lot with her parents, but everything was different. She wasn't just going on vacation—she was getting ready for a new reality and a new life.

Amelia took a bunch of clothes from a shelf, put them on her bed, and started going through them. After an hour, she got tired and went downstairs to the kitchen for a cup of tea.

Lucrecia was sitting in the living room with a laptop on a coffee table. "I found a direct flight from São Paulo to London the day after tomorrow in the morning," she said when she saw Amelia. "There is an earlier flight, tomorrow at ten forty in the evening, but it has an overnight layover in Amsterdam and is eight hours longer in total."

"I see..."

"The prices are higher than usual because Christmas is coming, but I don't want to delay it anyway. Come over here and take a look," Lucrecia urged her.

Amelia sat on the couch next to her mother, who showed her the computer screen with an opened flight-aggregation website.

"I would really prefer to depart earlier, but the prospect of spending twenty hours on a plane instead of eleven is not very appealing... What do you think?" asked Lucrecia.

"I really don't know..." said Amelia hesitantly. "I guess we could wait till the day after tomorrow. It's unlikely that one night would bring any dramatic changes, and we would travel in comfort and have more time to prepare this way."

"You're right," agreed Lucrecia. "I believe that's

the best option. We will go to São Paulo tomorrow in the afternoon and spend a night there, and you can pick up whatever you might need from our apartment."

"Sounds good."

"How is it going with your preparations? Do you think you will be ready by the end of the day?"

"Yes, I think so."

Amelia proceeded to the kitchen, then she heard a landline phone ringing in the living room, which was a rare occasion.

Lucrecia answered the call. "Hello. No, I'm afraid you can't. Yes, she is all right—thanks for your concern—but she is busy, and she won't be available anytime soon. I'm really sorry, Marcelu, but I can't help you. Have a nice day."

"Was that Marcelu?" asked Amelia, approaching her mother. "What did he want?"

"He wanted to talk to you and wasn't happy to accept no for an answer," scoffed Lucrecia.

"Why couldn't you pass me the phone? I was right here!" protested Amelia.

Lucrecia gave her a stern look. "I thought we have decided that you're staying away from him."

"Yes, but I could tell him about it myself," said Amelia with well-concealed indignation.

"I just saved you time. We don't have much left."

"All right, Mom. Thank you," Amelia sighed and went back to her room.

She started sorting through clothes piled on the bed again but then stopped, went to the desk, and opened and turned on her laptop.

She found an email from their schoolteacher and copied the address she needed from the list.

> *Hi Marcelu,*
>
> *I know that you tried to reach me, but my mom didn't pass me the phone. I'm sorry. She is just stressed out and doesn't want me to contact any of the locals.*
>
> *You've probably already heard about what happened this morning and my new circumstances.*
>
> *But in case you have something important to say, you have my ear.*
>
> *Sincerely, Amelia*

She clicked Send and returned to the sorting process. A pile of things was almost ready to go: changes of clothes for a few days, jeans, long-sleeved shirts, and sweaters.

Amelia woke her computer up from sleep mode and saw a new email from Marcelu:

> *Hi Amelia,*
>
> *Yes, I heard about it, and I am very sorry that your ordeal is not over yet. I really hate that this all happened to you at once, and I will do anything possible to help you.*
>
> *Actually, that's why I called you. I have*

some tentative information regarding your kidnapping attempt, which I heard from my friend. I will tell my dad about it, but I thought you may also want to know it.

I was lucky to get a security camera record that captured a vehicle that looked very similar to that Volkswagen van, and I got its plate number: BFA 7861.

Of course, there is no guarantee, but it might be a clue.

Stay safe and tell me if there is anything else I can do for you.

Yours Faithfully, Marcelu

Amelia pondered for a while. *Can I trust Marcelu?* she asked herself. He seemed to be very helpful, but at the same time, the fact that he'd found that record so quickly seemed suspicious. *If not Marcelu, then who?* Her parents obviously didn't take her seriously if they were keeping her in the dark about everything somehow important going on around her. She had a couple of friends at her old São Paulo school, but she wasn't so close with them that she would trust them with this disturbing story. Charlotta could be an option, but she was already scared enough by what had happened, and stressing her out even more would be no good. She needed a badass yearning for troubles rather than trying to avoid them. And she had only one match for these requirements: Marcelu.

Amelia spent another hour in consideration then

composed another email:

> *I really appreciate your help, and I would like us to have a more detailed discussion of what happened.*
>
> *Please, meet me this midnight at the bus station. Come alone and don't tell anybody that you are going to meet me. I'm relying on your integrity. It's very important. Wait for me near the entrance. I'll see you there.*

CHAPTER FIVE

MARCELU STOOD IN THE SPOT OF LIGHT from a street lamp near the shabby concrete two-story building that was Lindageral's bus station. He looked attentively into the darkness and listened to the silence occasionally interrupted by the sounds of cars passing by and dogs barking somewhere in the distance. The ticket office was already closed, and the station was almost empty, save for a few people.

He spun around when somebody touched his arm from behind.

"Hey, it's just me." Amelia grinned.

"Amelia!" He stared at her, surprised by her unusual outfit.

She was wearing a bulky gray hoodie with the hood over a red baseball cap, which hid her hair and part of her face. She also had black leggings and runners and a big orange-and-gray backpack on her shoulder, chock full.

"I see you are going to a baseball competition."

"Oh yeah, a baseball bat is something I might need." Amelia smirked and looked around to make sure that nobody else was nearby. "Did you bring what I asked you for?"

"Yes, here." He took a cell phone from his pocket. "It's primitive but very reliable, and the battery can last for almost a week, and it even has a camera. I guess that's what you need."

"Yes, exactly," agreed Amelia.

"And here is a prepaid SIM card. It has twenty-five reais on its account. I guess that's enough for now. I didn't activate it. You'd better do that yourself."

"Thanks a lot. How much do I owe you?" asked Amelia, putting the phone and the card away in the front pocket of her hoodie.

"Don't worry about it. It's my old phone. It was in a drawer for years, and I would probably never use it, so just take it."

"So, twenty-five reais, then. I only have fifty-real banknotes."

"Let's make a deal. Come back safe and take me somewhere for dinner." Marcelu smiled his most charming smile.

"If you wish so," agreed Amelia.

"So, where exactly are you going, may I ask?"

"I can't tell you. I don't know, myself."

Marcelu looked at her with disbelief.

"I just want to get lost. I'm taking a bus to Guaratinguetá right now just because it's the only one I can take right now and get out of here somewhere. Once I get there, I will decide what to do next. I'll take the next available transit to get to the next point until I get far enough from here. And then I'll stop at some nice place and lie low for a while."

"I see... Are you afraid of the troubles with police?" asked Marcelu cautiously.

"I'm not afraid of anything. I'm just fed up with being a puppet, not knowledgeable of what the hell is going on around me and unable to make my own decisions. I need some time with myself to think about everything," said Amelia with indignation. "I am supposed to go to Britain tomorrow, but I can't. I just can't. There's so much going on here, and I feel like I need to be here. I want to know who the hell those people who tried to kidnap me and broke into our house are, as well as what they want. I think my parents have an idea about it, but they would never discuss it with me—like I'm not a part of it, just an object without my own mind. It's so frustrating when you have no control of your own life. Do you understand me?"

"I think I do." Marcelu nodded.

"I trust you with keeping everything I just told you secret."

"Of course. You have my word. And yet, are you sure this is the only way? Your parents will probably go mad from worrying. And you may be putting yourself in real danger."

"Life is always full of risks, and they will always

worry about me, so what should I do, lock myself up at home just to keep them calm?"

"Maybe you could talk to them and discuss your decision."

"You think I didn't try? You don't know my parents. It always ends the same way—my mom brainwashing me and explaining just how inept and incapable of making any sane decisions I am. Don't get me wrong—I know that my mom is great, but she is also stubborn and relentless, always wanting everything to be done her way. So it's easier for me to just sneak out rather than telling my mom that I want to stay in Brazil and live by myself, listening to her derogatory rant, and then leaving home anyway. I left a note for them, and I will send them messages from time to time to let them know I'm safe and sound."

"So, you are absolutely determined? Aren't you afraid at all?"

"I believe I am able to throw the people hunting me off the trail. If I don't know where I am going, how would they know? I won't use my name and will try to blend in. And I believe that I myself am not what they need. I'm just an obvious and easy target to get to my father. Once I get off their radar, they will have no interest in me."

"Let's hope so. Dammit, I guess I'll be the first one under fire after you go missing. Your mother already suspects me. But that's fine. I'll survive it."

"I'm sorry," said Amelia, "and I really appreciate your help. I had nobody else to turn to. Be very careful when you go back today."

"Don't worry about me. Take care of yourself.

I hope you know what you're doing. Try not to get in trouble. In case you do, I want you to have this." He drew from his pocket a heavy folding knife with a khaki handle and handed it to Amelia.

"Huh... looks serious."

"Army rescue knife, assisted opening," Marcelu said.

Amelia took the knife after some hesitation. "Cool, now I'm armed!"

"Sure... I mean, you can use it to cut some firewood, peel potatoes. Think of me while doing this." Marcelu winked.

"I sure will."

"Be very cautious, please. Stay out of trouble, and don't try to be a hero if it gets tough. Remember, you have somewhere to return to. Here is my number." He handed her a folded piece of paper. "Call me any time of day or night if you need help."

"Thank you. That's very nice of you," she said, slightly embarrassed. "Oh, it looks like my bus. I gotta go. Don't go with me. We shouldn't be seen together."

She gave Marcelu a brief hug and headed to the bus stop.

Two more passengers were waiting for that bus, a young guy with earbuds in his ears and an older man who didn't pay any attention to her.

"How much to Guaratinguetá?" Amelia asked the driver as she hopped on the bus, trying to sound natural, like she had done it thousand times before, and it was just another trip for her.

"Seventeen reais."

She handed him a fifty-real bill, got back a ticket and change, and sat at a window in the middle of the bus. That was the first time she was taking a trip somewhere out of town alone, and the thought gave her a rather pleasant thrill. She was taking the first step of a big, exciting journey that could lead her anywhere.

The bus moved along a dark, almost empty highway, making stops from time to time to pick up more late-night travelers.

After the forty-minute trip, the bus stopped at the Guaratinguetá bus terminal, a big contemporary building of glass and concrete with an orange roof and a sign saying Rodoviaria. Amelia followed people inside the station, which was quiet and almost empty at that time of night. She explored a bus schedule on a wall and found that the next bus, to Piquete, departed at 5:27 a.m. The time was only one, so she had to wait for almost four and a half hours, which was a nuisance, and the station was closed for a night.

Hanging around the station was no good, and staying in one place would risk attracting unwanted attention, so Amelia decided to go for a walk. The night was warm, and the streets nearby were illuminated, so she didn't expect it to be unpleasant.

She walked around the station and turned onto the street that looked most appealing to her. In darkness, the city seemed to have some resemblance to Lindageral, tight rows of low-rise buildings with orange roof tiles, tile-paved sidewalks, but not as tidy and well-kept. Litter on the ground, low-hanging power lines, and shabby, discolored street signs significantly spoiled the impression.

Farther from the station, streets looked much more spectacular. She passed by a cathedral in colonial style and went through a historical district up to the river looping around the city, Paraíba do Sul, and walked down the bridge connecting President Vargas Avenue with Juscelino Kubitschek Avenue on the opposite side.

Amelia stood for a while on the bridge, contemplating the brown water of the river flowing steadily on its way, with patches of reflected light on the surface. Everything was quiet, and she felt like the only waking person in the sleeping city. She zigzagged her way through the not-so-picturesque residential part of Guaratinguetá—houses surrounded by tall concrete-and-steel fences and sparse vegetation—to the square in the center of the city, where all the roads converged like the spokes of a bicycle wheel, the University District.

The walk took her over an hour, and feeling fatigue in her legs, she found a bench in a park to rest on. Saving her energy would probably be better, as she had no idea where the dawning day would take her and what challenges it would bring, but even aware of this, she couldn't stay in one place.

Some vague anguish in her chest wanted her to keep going, even though her body was exhausted.

Amelia lay down on a bench and put her backpack under her head. She closed her eyes and sank into a light doze, her mind still aware of what was going on but free of any thoughts. After a while, her body got stiff from lying crooked on a hard surface, and she had to shift to a sitting position. She looked at her watch—only 3:45 a.m., still quite early. She sat for a minute, not moving, letting herself wake up completely. Then she stood up, did a bit of stretching, placed the backpack on her shoulder, and hit the road back to the bus terminal, trying to follow the same route she'd taken before.

The sun was dawning already, and its first dim light exposed the still empty and silent streets of Guaratinguetá to Amelia's view. Never before in her life had she been awake at that time. She'd neither woken up so early nor stayed up for so long. She felt strange, as if she was seeing the world from a different side.

She made a few loops around the station to arrive no earlier than twenty minutes before the departing time of the bus she aimed to take.

People were already lining up at the bus bay, and she joined them, keeping her head low and trying to avoid eye contact with anybody.

The bus arrived on time. Amelia paid fifty-six reais to get to Piquete, picked a spot at the rear of the bus at a window, and leaned against its glass, her elbow resting on the backpack on her knees.

Her parents still hadn't found out she'd left home. They must have still been asleep. This thought was both calming and disturbing, as if the point of no return was still ahead. Meanwhile, the bus wheeling its way down the highway was taking her closer to that point with every second.

At five minutes before seven, the bus arrived at its destination. Piquete's bus station consisted of two one-story red brick buildings covered by a roof made of metal trusses supported by pillars. The waiting area with chairs was under the roof between two buildings.

The view of the town was a sheer delight for the eye—a stretch of white red-roofed houses drowning in abundant vegetation, snugly placed amongst green hills and round-topped mountains.

With some regret, Amelia noted to herself that she couldn't settle here. The town was too small, and a newcomer would inevitably stick out among locals. Moreover, finding accommodations and a job would be hard.

She took a roadmap out of her backpack and unfolded it. It seemed like the optimal destination for her next trip could be Itajubá, in the state of Minas Gerais, a big enough city within a proximity of a two-hour drive, or in case that didn't meet her expectations, Pouso Alegre could be the next possibility.

"Excuse me, how can I get to Itajubá from here?" Amelia asked an elderly woman who'd gotten off the bus with her.

"Itajubá? I don't think there are buses going there," answered the woman, looking at Amelia with curiosity. "Where are you from?"

"I-I'm from Pindamonhangaba, going to visit my friends in Itajubá, but it seems like I made a mistake and took the wrong bus," she improvised.

"It looks like you really did," agreed the woman.

"You could take a bus to Cruzeiro from here or go back to Guaratinguetá. You will have more options there."

"Oh... All right, thanks."

The next bus to Cruzeiro was scheduled only at 1:00 a.m., and the prospect of waiting that long again wasn't encouraging, and going back to Guaratinguetá wasn't an option. The obvious solution was to get to the highway and try to get a ride. She'd never done anything like that before, and the idea made her slightly nervous, but almost everything she was doing was something she had never done before, after all. It was just one more step in her journey, she decided.

Using the map for reference, she made her way to Highway 459, going north to Minas Gerais up to Poços de Caldas.

Not much traffic was on the road. A couple of cars passed her by after she waved to them, but eventually a semitruck with the words Auto Parts stopped for her.

"Hey, jump in!" the driver shouted to her.

Amelia opened the door and jumped onto the footboard. "Hello. I'm going to Itajubá. Could you give me a ride?"

"Sure. I'm passing Itajubá on my way. It's more fun to have company," said the driver, a man of indefinable age somewhere between thirty and fifty, with sunburnt skin.

"Awesome!" Amelia sat in the passenger seat and fastened the seat belt.

"So why are you going to Itajubá? Anything interesting going on there?"

"There should be some events for Christmas, but I mostly just want to see my friends who live there."

"Not bad, not bad... So, you live in Piqueta? Nice little village, eh?"

"Oh yes, it's nice, indeed. It just gets boring there sometimes."

"I'm sure there's not much for girls your age to do. A big city is more fun."

Amelia hastened to change the subject. "What about you? Where do you live?"

"I live in Volta Redonda, it's in Rio de Janeiro state, but I travel for work all around Rio de Janeiro, São Paulo, and Minas Gerais, sometimes to Espírito Santo."

"It must be an exciting life," said Amelia with sincere enthusiasm.

"Kinda," agreed the driver. "You get tired sometimes, but I'm not complaining. I like speed, and this life is good for me. What do you do for life?"

Amelia quickly said the first thing that occurred to her. "Um... I work at my dad's grocery store. Not so exciting."

"Wanna be a truck driver too?" The man smirked.

"I'll think about it."

"I have a daughter. She's sixteen and just as restless as you. You must be a badass to go hitchhiking like this. Are you not afraid at all?"

"Only thing I'm afraid of is fear," said Amelia, mimicking the tone of an action hero.

"Ha! I'm Pedro, by the way. What's your name?"

"Maria." She couldn't come up with anything more

creative.

The road to Itajubá took about an hour and half, during which Pedro told her a lot of interesting stories that had happened to him on the road, and "Maria" maintained the conversation by complaining about intrusive customers coming into her store from time to time.

"Where in Itajubá do you want me to leave you? What's your friends' address?" asked Pedro when they were approaching the city.

"They live not far from the city center." Amelia knew absolutely nothing about Itajubá and was desperately inventing some generic answer. "Just leave me where it's convenient for you. I'll call my friends, and they will meet me."

CHAPTER SIX

PEDRO MADE A QUICK STOP AND dropped Amelia off near the intersection of five roads. Amelia thanked him and jumped out onto the pavement. The sun was shining bright, and the day was getting hot already, so she took off her hoodie and tied its sleeves around her waist and put on sunglasses.

She looked around and turned down one of the narrow streets that crossed the highway where Pedro had gone. She chose the road on a whim and walked down the narrow tiled pavement. The street had low-rise commercial buildings on both sides, most of them just concrete boxes with very plain and practical design, no architectural delights. From time to time, palms or Pernambuco trees fit in small spots of soil among the concrete.

The street smoothly turned into a bridge over a small river that flowed unobtrusively between buildings. On the other side of the river, the view changed slightly, including more historical buildings with scenic architecture, which were not so cramped, interspersed with green frontages. Some high-rises appeared along Amelia's way as she followed the road uphill. She assumed that must have been a more central and lively part of the city.

Near a white chapel on a hill, the road turned into a small roundabout, and Amelia took the street in the middle, considering a blue building fitted into the acute angle formed by forking streets, with white balusters and pediments, a decorative mansard roof, and white platbands of windows, shadowed by similar white marquises. The house was adorned with a bougainvillea covered with pink flowers growing near its wrought-iron railings.

Amelia followed farther along the street and, after three blocks, ended up on a big square shadowed by tall plane trees, with lots of benches, fountains in the middle, and a stage with a spherical white concrete hood over it. It looked like a perfect place to linger and rest for a while. Lots of small cafes and stores surrounded the square, and she went to check them out.

The time was still quite early, a quarter before nine, and most of the places were still closed, but she was lucky enough to find an open coffee shop just around a corner. She got a ham-and-cheese sandwich, coffee with cream in a paper cup, and a local newspaper with advertisements and went back to the square to sit on a bench and have her breakfast while observing Itajubá's life going on around her.

Fatigue and hunger, which had been suppressed by adrenaline till then, finally caught up to her, and she took a big bite of the sandwich. Everything around seemed to be calm and peaceful. Birds chirped in the shadows of the trees. A woman with a music player in her waist bag and headphones in her ears was going for her morning jog, a couple of senior men were sitting on a bench and discussing something, and a man was walking a dog.

When Amelia finished her breakfast and slowly walked around the square, she heard an angry man screaming something at a woman, who stood across from the windows of a café with a boutique next to it.

"Get out of here, you whore! You have no shame to stand here in broad daylight!"

"Hey, senhor, I'm not doing anything wrong! I was just going to do some painting."

Amelia went closer. The woman had a wheeled cart and a portable wooden easel with a canvas, on which she'd already made an outline of the building she was facing.

"Go do your paintings elsewhere, *puta*!" A burly man wearing an apron stepped out of the cafe's doorway and approached her.

"But Senhor Rodrigues asked me to make a painting of the café!" protested the woman.

"Rodrigues is not in charge here. I am! And I'm

telling you to get out of here with your daub. Nobody is paying you for it and never would!"

"Hey! I'm not in your territory. It's a public place. You can't tell me to leave!"

"I don't need a streetwalker loitering around my place!" the man shouted, his round face turning red. "Go to Alcanzar Club or wherever your lot is hooking up clients."

"I'm not hooking anyone up, and you're not telling me what to do!" the woman hollered back. "This city is mine as much as it is yours!"

"I said get out!" bellowed the man and kicked her cart, flipping it over.

The woman gasped in a shock as canvas paintings, tubes of oil, and brushes scattered on the pavement.

The man turned around and walked away with a satisfied look on his face.

"Bastard!" the woman yelled at his back.

Amelia approached her. "Let me help you," she said and bent down to pick up scattered paintings and art supplies.

The woman, who'd frozen in place for a few seconds, looking angrily at the door that closed behind her offender, turned her head to Amelia.

She was not tall and rather sturdy, with wide shoulders and hips. Her thick curly hair was dyed dark ginger with overgrown roots revealing their natural black color. She was wearing a jean jumpsuit over a white tank top, which contrasted with her red sunburnt shoulders, covered with freckles, and the dirty white runners on her feet.

"Yeah... thanks," said the woman, unfreezing. She picked up a painting from the pavement and examined it.

"That man seems to be a complete jerk!" noted Amelia. "What's wrong with him?"

"Arr, he's just made of shit," spat the woman.

"Are those paintings yours?" asked Amelia, nodding at the canvas on the cart.

"Yep."

"They are very beautiful."

"You really think so? Most people think they're ugly."

"Yeah..." Amelia examined several paintings chaotically piled up in a cart, mostly landscapes and abstractions, abundant with bright saturated colors. "I mean... I know it's a wrong compliment to make to an artist," she went on. "A piece of art doesn't have to be beautiful. It should be meaningful, first of all. It can be realistic, evocative, emotional. As long as it conveys what an artist meant to show, it's good."

"Hmm... thanks. You sound like an expert."

"I'm not one, not really, but I like art. I see you perform mostly in the postimpressionist style, or is modernism closer to you?"

"What? I don't even know what these words mean." The painter laughed.

"Where did you learn how to draw?"

"Nowhere. I just watched a TV show about that famous woman artist, what's her name... Anita Malfatti! And I thought it would be fun to try. I bought some oil paint and canvas in a supermarket and started to paint. I love it. It distracts me from everything.”

“Wow, that’s great. You’re a natural talent!” exclaimed Amelia.

“Heh heh, thanks. Do you want to buy a painting from me? Just a hundred reais for each!”

“I’d love to, but I’m afraid I have no place to hang them,” said Amelia.

“Eighty,” offered the woman.

“No, I mean it, I really can’t—at least, not now.”

“Whatever you can offer for this. I’ll take anything,” blurted the painter with a note of despair in her voice.

“Listen. I seriously can’t. I just arrived in this city, and I’m looking for a place to stay. I don’t want to damage your fine picture, carrying it around for a whole day.”

“Oh, I see,” sighed the woman. She took a pack of cigarettes out of her belly bag, lit one of them, and took a drag with her hands slightly shaking. Amelia noticed her arms were covered in multiple scars as from small cuts.

“Believe me, I really like your paintings and would like to buy at least one when I have somewhere to hang them,” Amelia assured her. “By the way, maybe you know someone who sublets a room?” asked Amelia.

The woman considered her for a moment.

“I have a space in my apartment. Not sure if you’d like it. It’s very shabby and near the industrial zone. But you could stay tonight if you don’t have anywhere else to go.”

“Oh great!” Amelia rejoiced. “I’m not very picky. Do you live alone?”

"Mostly. But I have guests from time to time. We play music and get loud."

"It's not a problem for me at all."

"Cool. My name is Fortunata, by the way. What's your name?"

"Am... Paola!"

"Very well, Paola. I'm heading home now with all this stuff. Do you want to go with me?"

"Yes, for sure!"

***

Robert was working at his computer when Lucrecia burst into the room, outraged.

"Amelia's gone!"

"What? Gone where?" asked Robert, confused.

"I was wondering if she'd slept in and went to her bedroom, and there's no sign of her, just her clothes scattered on the bed and this note on a table." She handed him a lined piece of paper ripped out of a notepad.

Mom and Dad,

After some consideration, I decided not to go to London. Too many things are going on around here to just ignore them.

I want to live by myself for a while and see what I am capable of.

Don't worry about me. I will be safe. And don't try to find me. As long as nobody, including you, knows my whereabouts, I am safe from whoever means harm to our family.

Amelia

"Oh dear." Robert sighed.

"This girl has lost her bearings completely! What does she think she is doing? She has never stayed by herself a single day in her life!" Perplexed, Lucrecia stretched her arms out.

"Well, there should be a first time for everything, so maybe it's time for her," said Robert.

His wife looked at him in disbelief. "Are you serious? *Now* is absolutely not a good time for it, when somebody is conspiring against us. I don't understand how you can be so calm!" she exclaimed.

Robert put his hands on her shoulders.

"Carinho, keeping calm is the first thing we should take care of. I believe Amelia is not in immediate danger right now, and we have time to consider what happened and what can we do."

"How can you be so sure? Why would she decide all of a sudden to run away from home? I'm sure somebody put her up to it! What if it was a trap?"

"I believe that our daughter is a smart and sensible girl, and she wouldn't fall into a trap so easily," said Robert reassuringly. "Let's go downstairs. I'll make you a cup of coffee or tea. You are all shaking from agitation. You need to calm down."

Lucrecia raised her arms in speechless exasperation then dropped them and exhaled. "All right."

They went to the kitchen, where Lucrecia loaded

the coffee machine, taking over from her husband, in an attempt to get her hands and mind busy with something.

"That boy, Marcelu... I'm sure it was him! I knew that was something wrong about him. He tried to call Amelia yesterday, but I didn't allow him to talk to her. Obviously, he found a way to lure her away from home." Lucrecia continued her reasoning while the coffee machine hissed. "If he is in league with that gang of kidnappers, Amelia is in serious trouble!"

"Hold on!" Robert raised his hand. "We can't accuse people without any evidence!"

"Are you going to do anything at all?" Lucrecia burst out.

"Of course. We will talk to Marcelu. He is our daughter's friend and might know something. He and that girl... What's her name?"

"Charlotta. She's a very nice girl. Her mom is a seamstress, and her dad is a tractor driver. He works for us. I'm not worried about her. She couldn't be any bad influence on Amelia. Unlike that Marcelu boy."

"For sure, we will talk to Marcelu first and also with Diego. But for Christ's sake, let's refrain from any accusations for now! It would just make everything worse. We need people to cooperate with us, so better not to alienate them."

"Yes, you are right." Lucrecia sighed. She took a bottle of rum out of a cabinet and added some to her coffee.

"I'm so sorry I was too immersed in work last time and might have gotten out of touch with you and

Amelia," said Robert apologetically. "Did you have any disagreements with her recently?"

Lucrecia shook her head. "Nothing major. Yesterday, we mostly discussed the travel details with her." She took a sip.

"I believe Amelia will come back soon. She just needs to let off some steam. Too many things have happened to her recently. No wonder she couldn't deal with all this pressure."

"Pressure, huh?" scoffed Lucrecia. "This girl has a miracle life. I wish my parents could've taken me to London when I was eighteen. When I was her age, I had to work delivering newspapers and helping in a print shop and serving tables in the daytime while studying at college in the evenings! That's what I call pressure, not the annoyance of a spoiled little girl not feeling appreciated enough."

"Oh yes, I remember meeting you at that reception at the newspaper office where you worked as a server." Robert smiled. "Thank God you were there, or we would probably never have met otherwise. São Paulo is too big. You were amazing—so confident, bright, and independent. And you still are, of course."

A weak smile cracked Lucrecia's face.

"Right, that fateful event. Your arrogant friend asked my opinion about investing in stocks, trying to make fun of a waitress while I was pouring him a drink."

"Yes, and it was fun to see Romero's face when you said something like 'If I were you, I would invest in the Brazilian stock market. Even though it may seem stagnant now, it's going to go up in a few years because President Collor's "Plano Real" is working and bringing the inflation down whereas the Asian market collapse is going to strike most of the leading economies hard.' It was fabulous! I'll never forget it. And as time has proven, your estimate was accurate."

"He chose the wrong object for his joke. I didn't just deliver newspapers. I also read them," said Lucrecia, and they both burst into laughter.

CHAPTER SEVEN

WHILE HER HUSBAND MADE A PHONE call, Lucrecia finished her coffee.

"I arranged a meeting with Diego at eleven a.m. at his home," Robert said. "His son will be there. He is standing by Marcelu and asserting that he had nothing to do with Amelia's escapade."

"No wonder," scoffed Lucrecia skeptically.

"And," emphasized Robert, "he says they have new information pushing forward the investigation of the attempted kidnapping."

"I really hope they do, for their own sake, because I believe it's beyond their level and it's federal police who should work with this case."

"Federal police will get involved soon," Robert assured her. "Diego wants to share this with us confidentially, for the sake of our old friendship. Legally, they are not supposed to give away this information to anyone, including us, while the investigation is in progress."

"All right. I'll get ready."

She showered and dressed in wide black trousers and a white blouse from the latest collection of a famous designer and put on her makeup and perfume as if trying to show that she was still a decision maker who should be taken seriously.

At eleven, Lucrecia parked her silver Audi at the curb near the police chief's house and headed toward the gate, hand in hand with her husband, who hadn't bothered to change from the casual light cotton pants and T-shirt he'd been wearing at home.

"Lucrecia, Robert, please come in!" said Diego Campras, opening the gate for them.

They followed him in through the open front door.

"Celestia, get off!" he yelled at an Airedale terrier that started barking at them.

"My wife is on shift at the hospital. It's only me and my son." He nodded at Marcelu, who was entering the living room. "I guess you haven't met my son recently, Robert?"

"No, I haven't had a chance," he answered. "Last time I saw him, he wasn't as tall. Nice to see you again, my friend."

Robert stretched out his hand and patted the boy on the shoulder.

"I'm glad to see you, too, Senhor Robert. Sorry

that the occasion is not very happy, though."

"Just 'Robert,' please. Things are tough, indeed, but hopefully, with your help, we can get it settled."

"Are you hungry?" asked Diego. "We have *farofa* for lunch, from yesterday's dinner."

"Thank you, but let's talk business first," said Lucrecia firmly.

"For sure. You want to come to my office?"

All four of them proceeded to Diego's home office, a small room on the second floor. Diego turned on a computer facing the entrance.

"Please, have a seat." He offered Lucrecia his soft rolling chair, which she accepted, and sat next to her in a small foldable chair, turning it to face her.

Diego initiated the conversation, joining his fingertips in a pose of a patient listener. "So, your daughter left home last night?"

"Yes," Robert and Lucrecia answered synchronously.

"We checked our CCTV records and figured out that she left at eleven thirty-five," said Robert. "Lucrecia was asleep already, and I was working in my office but didn't hear anything. She took only her hiking backpack with her."

"She left a note," said Lucrecia, taking a sheet of paper out of her purse and handing it to Diego.

"So, I believe that everything is indicating that she left home willingly, without any coercion, and isn't at immediate risk of harm," concluded the police chief after scanning it quickly. "And she has already reached the age of majority, so there are no legitimate reasons to declare her missing."

Lucrecia nodded. "Yes, we are well aware of this. But as you realize, it doesn't make us less worried about our only child, who has gone off in some unknown direction. She left all her IDs at home, and she doesn't have a phone. And there are people clearly willing to harm her!" She took a deep breath to compose herself.

"Could she go to her friends or relatives?" asked Diego.

"I talked to my sister, who lives in São Paulo. She will let us know if Amelia comes by, which is unlikely. My parents live in Portugal, and we don't have other close relatives here. Robert has a couple cousins, but we don't really keep in touch with them. Robert sends them greetings on major holidays, but I don't even have their addresses or phone numbers, and neither does she."

"Regarding friends, I have the numbers of a couple of her best friends in São Paulo, and I will get in touch with them as well. First, I want to have a word with her friends here, in Lindageral. Including your son." Lucrecia gave Marcelu a questioning look. "I believe you were someone she was spending a lot of time with recently, besides Charlotta. Did she share any of her plans with you?"

Marcelu shook his head. "I wouldn't say it was a lot of time. Actually, that time we went to ride horses together was our only one-on-one time. And she never did confide in me. Why would she? I believe you should talk to Charlotta. She may know more. And Andrea, our other classmate Amelia was friends with."

"We will consider this. Thank you," said Lucrecia. "Meanwhile, we have decided not to advertise the fact that Amelia left home. So please, don't tell anyone."

"Yes, if this news spreads, it will eventually reach her intended kidnappers," explained Robert. "We don't want them to figure out that she is somewhere out there alone and vulnerable."

"That totally makes sense," agreed Diego. "We keep our mouths shut, right, Son?"

"Of course. That is very serious. I don't want to put Amelia's life in danger," said Marcelu solemnly.

"Very good. We knew we could rely on you." Robert nodded at him in approval. "Now, can we talk about the investigation? What is that new information you have?"

"I rode around the town early in the morning after the graduation party," started Marcelu. "I drove to all the gas stations on all the roads leading out of Lindageral and asked service workers to check CCTV records for the white van with a broken left taillight, for a small reward. And I was lucky enough to recognize the vehicle that the bandits used after checking the third gas station, on the road leading south, just near the edge of the town."

"Oh, great!" exclaimed Robert. "What a smart idea!"

"Dad, could you please open the snapshots on your computer?" asked Marcelu.

"Here, I'll show you," Diego clicked on a folder and opened a slightly pixelated but distinct enough picture of a vehicle and scrolled through a few more. "Here, we got his number." He pointed at an enlarged picture with the license plate.

"Perfect," exclaimed Robert, typing the number into his phone.

"We already checked out this number," said Diego. "Here, look." He opened a sheet of vehicle registration data. "It belongs to Stallion Logistics, a company registered in São Paulo three months ago. I haven't found much about this company. They don't have a website and don't advertise themselves. It seems pretty much like it's fake. We are trying to figure out information about the owner."

Robert thought for a moment. "I think I know how to find out. I have a person working with company registration and have access to the database." He quickly searched for a number on his phone. "If you excuse me, I'll just make one quick call. Could you print this out for me, please?"

Diego sent the information to his laser printer, and in a few seconds, it spat out the sheet.

"Thank you." Robert took the paper from the tray and quickly scanned it while listening to the ringtone on his phone. "Anita, good morning! How's life?... I'm also not so bad. Are you at work now? Do you mind if I take a couple moments of your precious time? I need some information. I'll make it up for you, be sure... Yes, I have all the registration numbers." He spelled out all the requested information. "Yes, for sure, you can call me back." He hung up and winked at Marcelu, who was watching him with interest. "It's good to know people."

After a couple minutes, his phone rang.

"Yes, Andrea, any news? Oh... Is it for sure? Okay, thank you. You helped me a lot."

Robert finished the call and stood with a perplexed expression on his face while the three other people in the room gazed at him in expectation.

Diego broke the silence. "So, what's the news? Come on, fire it up. We're all in the same boat here. You can share it with us."

"This Stallion Logistics is a subsidiary of Lacerdo Motors Company," said Robert, turning to his wife with a distinct vexation on his face.

"Oh, that's interesting! How come they got involved?" Diego exclaimed.

"Lando, what a bastard!" hissed Lucrecia. "He ate and drank at our table."

"I was wondering which one of them. He was the second one I suspected." Robert rubbed his nose.

"Would you mind giving us a little heads up?" suggested Diego.

Robert exchanged looks with Lucrecia then turned to him.

"I'd like to, but it's a complicated and somewhat sensitive matter... I'm not sure if I can involve you in this, for the sake of your own safety. I was wary to share it even with my wife."

Diego cleared his throat. "I understand that I am just a small-town cop busy with the paperwork of petty thefts and drunken fights, something far below what a statesman and politician like you is bothered with. But you can fully trust in me, as I am your old friend, and you can be certain of my impartiality, as I'm of no interest to any of your opponents, being such a small fry."

"I didn't mean to offend you, you know." Robert sighed wearily and made eye contact with Lucrecia.

Her expression told him, *"Do as you will. I already have no freaking idea of what we should do."*

Robert looked back at Diego, pointed at the younger Campras with his eyes, and raised his eyebrows.

"About my son, you can trust him no less than me," said Diego, grabbing his son by the shoulders. "Never mind that he is only eighteen. He is smarter than many much older people. He pays attention to things no one else would notice and always knows when to speak and when to keep his mouth shut. Don't forget he is the one who came up with the idea of how to track that van."

"Very well. Diego, Marcelu, I appreciate your help, and I believe we need to employ all the resources we have. Let's have a seat, and I'll tell you the details."

***

"Here we are. This is my humble little abode." Fortunata opened the steel door of her apartment on the second floor of a ramshackle two-story building.

The staircase walls were shedding their paint, covered with marker writing. The heavy smell of cigarette smoke hung in the air, soaked into those ugly walls. Amelia admitted to herself that this devastation was beyond what she was prepared for. She was almost ready to turn around and leave in search of something better if it wouldn't have been utterly rude to her new friend.

However, the apartment looked much better inside. At least it seemed much cleaner and less stinky.

"Sorry the air is stale here. I don't have an air conditioner, and I shut the windows when I leave," explained Fortunata, dragging in her wheeled cart.

She went to a window and opened the red flower-patterned curtains, allowing sunlight into a room that was both kitchen and living room. A big striped mat lay on the floor near a dented ginger-brown couch, a low table, and unmatched chairs.

"Do you want something, coffee or tea?" asked Fortunata.

"Yes, if you were going to make yourself a cup. Otherwise, I don't want to disturb you," said Amelia, looking around.

Almost stainless, the white walls seemed to have been recently painted. The wall opposite the kitchen sink and stove was decorated with a couple of framed paintings and various music instruments hanging above the couch—a four-stringed cavaquinho, agogo bells, and chocalho shakers—and a tall atabaque drum stood on the floor.

"Are those instruments yours? I mean, do you play them?" asked Amelia.

"Just a little bit," answered her hostess. "I used to dance samba before. We still gather sometimes with friends and make some noise."

"No way! You're not just an artist. You're a dancer

as well! How many talents can one person have?"

Fortunata laughed. "I don't perform so often now. But I knew better days." She pointed at a picture of her with three other girls, wearing sparkling two-piece bikinis and colorful feathers on their heads.

"Why not?"

"Don't get many offers. I'm getting old and not so agile. There are lots of younger, fresher girls," she said bitterly.

Amelia looked at Fortunata in disbelief. "Sorry to hear that. It doesn't sound fair to me at all. How old are you, if you don't mind me asking?"

"I'm twenty-eight, almost twenty-nine. And you?"

"Eighteen."

"Darn, you are so young!"

"But I don't dance samba. I'm not competition for you anyway," said Amelia jokingly.

"Well, you could take a chance. Would be good for you. You're kinda too thin, just like a boy, but that's fine as long as you can shake it. I'll show you some moves if you want."

"Never thought about it, but maybe it could be an option for me," answered Amelia, slightly perplexed. "I'm new to this city and looking for any opportunities."

"Right, you told me. Where are you from?"

"São Paulo."

"Really? And what brought you here, to Itajubá?"

"It seems like a nice, calm place to stay. I had enough troubles in São Paulo."

"Like you're hiding from someone? Your

boyfriend?”

“Yes, mostly,” Amelia said, agreeing with this version. “And my mom. Sometimes, relationships with people around you get way too complicated.”

“I hear ya. My fiancé, Raul, and I also have a complicated relationship.”

“You have a fiancé? Does he live with you?” asked Amelia apprehensively.

“No, we don’t live together. He just stays here from time to time. He has a very hectic schedule. He trades stocks online.”

“Sounds cool.”

“Not so much. Mostly, he just loses all his money and gets into debt I have to pay for.”

“Oh.”

“Yeah, I know. He’s just a big dumbass. We’re fighting all the time. But I hope that one day I can make a decent man out of him and we will leave Itajubá and settle somewhere in the countryside, in our own house with a farm and kids.”

“You don’t like Itajubá? It seems nice to me so far,” said Amelia.

“Well... It’s not so bad. I used to live in much worse places. It’s just my personal dislike, I guess. My life turned into a mess since I moved here.”

“Sorry to hear...”

“Ugh... Anyway, enough about that. It looks like I’m complaining to you. I guess you have other things to do than listening to my whining.”

“That’s fine. We all need to complain from time to

time," Amelia reassured her. "And it's good to know more about each other."

"I'm not able to talk about it without a drink anyway. Makes me too unhinged."

Amelia nodded, not wanting to stir her up anymore.

"I was going to apply for some jobs advertised in the newspaper. Are you cool if I use your bathroom? I would like to take a shower and change my clothes first. I've been on the road for many hours and need some refreshment to make a good impression."

"Sure."

After some consideration, Amelia asked, "Actually, I was also thinking about getting a haircut. Are there any hairdressing salons nearby?" She figured changing her appearance as much as she could before going out and meeting people would be better. She didn't really think anybody outside Lindageral knew who she was, let alone being able to recognize her, but being cautious couldn't hurt.

"I have no idea, honestly. I always style my hair by myself and don't remember the last time I went to the hairdresser's. I could cut your hair if you don't want something super fancy."

"Oh, really? That would be awesome!" said Amelia, figuring the fewer people saw her original look, the better. "Can you do it right now?"

"Sure, why not? My plans for the day were kinda ruined, so hanging out with you is better than moping around."

Fortunata turned on a music radio station playing energetic music and took scissors out of a kitchen drawer. She brought a stool from the kitchen to the bathroom and placed it near the sink.

"Have a seat, Paola," she said.

Amelia sat down and untied her long hair. "I want it this long." She pointed at the middle of her neck.

"So short? Are you sure? Your hair is gorgeous, so silky and shiny."

"Yes. I think it's time for some changes."

"I hear you. Starting a new life, eh?"

Amelia nodded.

"Do you want it just straight?"

"I'd prefer some kind of a cascade, if that's possible."

"Nothing is impossible, sunshine! Ready? Let's rave!"

Fortunata started snapping her scissors, cutting off long strands of hair first then shaping what was left with more precise cuts.

"Here we go. What do you think?" she asked after making final adjustments.

"Awesome! You have a good hand," said Amelia, looking at her changed reflection in the mirror.

Fortunata smirked. "Glad you're not mad at me." She brought a broom with a dustpan and swept up the shreds of chestnut hair scattered on the floor.

Amelia took out a tube of semipermanent eggplant-colored hair dye she'd bought a long time before but hadn't gotten a chance to try out. Then she applied it to her hair, already having taken her T-shirt off, waited for fifteen minutes, and washed it off in the shower.

After she finished and dried her hair with a blow dryer, she evaluated the result in the mirror and was satisfied. She could hardly recognize her own reflection.

She applied charcoal-black eyeliner to her eyes to make her new identity differ from her regular self even more.

"I'm going out to do some job hunting," Amelia told Fortunata, who was watching TV in the kitchen. "There's a restaurant that's hiring temporary staff for Christmas events. Gonna try my luck."

"Which restaurant?"

"The Agave."

"Oh, I know that place. It's a block away from Santiago Square." Fortunata turned off the TV. "I can go with you so you don't get lost. You don't know the city yet."

"Oh, there's no need for that. I will be all right," Amelia assured her. "You've already spent a lot of time on me."

"I'm not in the mood to do anything else today, and I don't want to stay here alone. I can show you around if you want."

"Okay, then. Let's go!"

CHAPTER EIGHT

THEY WALKED FOR ABOUT HALF AN HOUR to get to the address Amelia had found in the newspaper. It was just a few blocks away from the square with fountains, a red-brick building with a terrace surrounded by a tall wooden lattice fence on the corner of two narrow streets.

Amelia turned the knob on the wicket and opened it. The girls entered the patio, shaded with brown tarpaulin canopy and rhododendron bushes blooming with orange flowers.

The time was already past noon, and few of the tables outside were occupied, although most of the guests preferred to sit indoors to retreat from the midday heat in the air-conditioned lounge.

"You go. I'll sit here and order something to drink

and maybe some food," decided Fortunata. "Do you like pizza? I'll order a large one so we can share. Which kind do you like?"

"Neapolitan or Hawaiian. Actually, you pick, I like all of them."

"Got it. I'll wait for you here," Fortunata said and sneaked to the table farthest from the entrance.

Amelia nodded and proceeded inside.

A hostess in a black shirt and matching black skirt welcomed her as she entered.

"Hello, I've read your ad regarding temporary helpers," explained Amelia.

"Right, very well. Follow me. I will introduce you to the owner."

They went around the bar counter into the staff-only zone. The hostess knocked on one of the doors and opened it.

"Here, Renata, this girl is offering us her help with the festive events."

"Thank you, Aline," said the imposing young woman with pitch-black hair, sitting at a white computer desk. She smiled at Amelia. "Come in, please."

Aline let her in and closed the door behind her. The office room was small and narrow, although the bright white of the walls, locker, desk, and window frame made the space seem less confined.

Amelia sat in the white folding chair for visitors. "Hello, my name is Paola. I'm looking for a job, and I would like to apply to the event helper position. I found your ad in the newspaper."

"Have you worked at the restaurant before?" asked Renata.

"No. I just finished school and have never worked before."

"Do you have a resume?"

"No... I didn't think about it. I don't have much to put in it. But I can make one."

"If you don't have one, that's fine. It just makes it easier to keep track of applicants." Renata intertwined her fingers, gracefully stretched them from side to side, and put her joined hands on her desk, displaying her black nail polish and a diamond ring on her left middle finger. "So, we are going to have a big event on Christmas Eve and on New Year's Eve as well, and we are fully booked this week. We need a couple more people to help us with event preparation, including delivery, kitchen assistance, and event cleanup. Are you physically fit enough to stay on your feet for many hours, move furniture, and carry heavy trays with food?"

"Yes, I am," said Amelia firmly. She hesitated, wondering if she should mention jiujitsu classes and going to the gym. "I lived on a farm and helped my parents with farm work, so it won't be much harder for me."

"Oh, really? I also grew up on a farm, not far from here. My parents still keep it. They love digging in soil and will never quit. I buy their veggies for the restaurant sometimes. But their lifestyle is not for me. I prefer city life, so I understand why you decided to hit Itajubá."

"Yep, I'm fed up with the countryside," confirmed Amelia.

"Welcome, and I hope the city will not disappoint you." Renata smiled at her.

"So, what do you think? Can you start today? I have a couple more people coming at two p.m. You could join them for a quick intro."

"Yes, that works for me," Amelia said, glad that the ordeal of her first job search was finished.

She hustled out to the patio to join Fortunata, who was already munching on a piece of generously cheesed pizza and sipping beer from a tall glass.

"How was it?" asked Fortunata.

"Great! Renata, the owner, is really cool. She said I can start today."

"Oh, that's quick! Congratulations!" Fortunata raised her glass.

"Thanks! The lunch is on me, as I'm employed now. I still have a few more hours left." Amelia sat on a chair across her and took a piece of pizza, as doing an interview had made her hungry.

"Let's drink to it! What do you drink?"

"I don't think that's a good idea. After work would be better."

"C'mon, Paola, just one drink—something light. It will wind away before you start. Which cocktail do you like? They make very good caipirinha."

"Never tried it."

Fortunata shook her head in disapproval. "If you are going to work in a restaurant, you should be an expert in booze." She waved at a waitress. "Two caipirinhas for us, please."

Admitting the failure of her objections, Amelia munched on another slice of pizza.

After a while, the girl brought them two highball glasses with sliced lime and crushed ice.

"To your success!" proclaimed Fortunata, raising a glass.

Amelia mirrored her move and took a sip through a straw. It tasted delightful. She had tried some cocktails at her São Paulo friends' parties, and her parents were quite loose about it, but she didn't have much interest in alcohol.

"Do you like it? It's cachaça, lime juice, and sugar. The trick is to mix the right amount of each. People used it as a remedy during a Spanish flu outbreak. I know everything about cocktails. I'll teach you."

"Did you work in a bar?"

"Yep, but not as a bartender." Fortunata smirked. "But I used to dance in many bars and clubs from Belo Horizonte to Rio and tasted everything they had on the drink menus."

"That sounds interesting! But how come you ended up here? You said you didn't like Itajubá."

"It's not the worst place I've had to live either." Fortunata took a long sip of her caipirinha. "I'm from Perdigão, the small town north of here. Bet you never heard of it... Nobody in the world knows about it. It's in the middle of nowhere. Even its name speaks for itself. It's lost from this world. Nothing ever happens there. I'd been dreaming of leaving it as long as I can remember. I wanted to be a dancer and perform at festivals and events.

Me and three other girls from my town joined a band and started performing in nightclubs nearby. We were really good. Then we got an invitation to Belo Horizonte and started making some money and could afford to rent a place for all four of us. Oh, it was an amazing time," she said with a nostalgic note.

"But it didn't last long. Soon, everything went awry. One of the girls, Clara, started thinking that she was too good for us and deserved better. She started getting bitchy with me and the other girls. We all started to fight and split up. One of the girls got married, and the other returned to her hometown. I continued to perform as often as I could, but I didn't get much money. So I went to Rio to take my chances there. I had nothing to lose anyway, but it was not much easier. Nobody knew me there. Still, I kept trying. I lowered my standards a bit and accepted invitations from places whose doorsteps I normally wouldn't cross. One night, I was dancing in a street club when I met Raul. He waited until I finished and then asked me for a drink. When you dance in clubs, there are always lots of guys swaying around you like flies, but he was different—so charming, so suave. He was just visiting friends in Rio. We spent all night together, and then he offered to take me with him. To Itajubá—that's where he was from."

"No way! You just met him and decided to leave with him?"

"Yeah, I was already head over heels into him! He said he'd help me to get a permanent job."

"But I guess it didn't go so smooth," said Amelia.

"No, not at all. I stayed at his place for a while, but the life he led was too messy for me. Partying all the time with his junky friends, scantily clad women, always those women..." Fortunata dropped her head into her palms. Then she raised it again and reached into her bag for a cigarette and a lighter. "Mind if I smoke?"

"No, that's fine," answered Amelia, looking at her with some concern.

Fortunata took a deep drag on her cigarette.

"So, you couldn't stay there any longer and left?" asked Amelia after a pause.

"Not just like that, but eventually, yes." Fortunata exhaled a cloud of smoke.

"Good for you!"

"Then he got back to me and promised he would quit living like that. He really tried. We started everything over again. All was good till I found him with one of his whores on the couch in my home. They both were on crack. I kicked them out somehow. I thought I might kill them." Fortunata took another drag, her hand shaking slightly.

"I was supposed to perform in a club that night. I was so worked up I could just roll on the floor and scream. Thank God, I had a bottle of rum, and it untied me after a shot or two so I was able to go to work. Better I didn't. There was a bitchy manager who didn't like me, and it was his shift that night. He smelled booze and started picking on me. I didn't drink that much. I wasn't even drunk! I was perfectly able to perform as good as always. Who doesn't drink in clubs at night, for Christ's sake?

Anyway, we had an awful fight, and they didn't invite me anymore."

"I'm so sorry to hear about that, Fortunata. That Raul seems to be a total jerk."

"Oh, he is such an idiot sometimes. He can be so sweet and cool when he wants, but then something clicks in his mind, and he starts being an idiot again. I've already learnt to recognize this pattern. If only I could learn how to keep him on the right track..." said Fortunata bitterly.

"Sounds like a lot of work. Are you sure that it's worth it?" asked Amelia cautiously.

"Who knows? I've tried to quit him many times, but something always pulled me back. It seems like we got so intertwined that we can never split, no matter what. Like it was written in heaven that we should be together, understand?"

Amelia nodded, suppressing a sigh. She was getting really worried about her new friend.

"He got in real trouble recently, owed money to people you don't want to cross your path. I helped him to pay his debt, and he was so grateful. I hope it showed him who he can trust in this life and who not. None of his so-called friends was up to it. They are only good to drink and do drugs together."

"So you two are together again?"

"Yep, and we're going to get married as soon as Raul finally figures his stuff out."

"I really hope everything will turn out well," said Amelia.

They finished their caipirinhas, and Fortunata

ordered another cocktail and Amelia coffee.

Some time was left before two, so they took a walk to a nearby park.

Amelia heard somebody saying her name and jerked her head in their direction before her brain was able to process the whole phrase from one of two men they passed by: "It's on Amelia Braga square, just a five-minute walk from here." She smiled to herself. Apparently, they loved her namesake princess in this city enough to have named a square after her.

"Do you have any ideas of pictures you want to paint?" she asked Fortunata, to switch her mind to something more positive after their emotional conversation. "It seems there are lots of beautiful locations around here."

Her artistic friend was eager to share her impressions of the city's views.

After a while, Amelia said, "It's time for me to start work. Thanks for spending time with me and showing me the city."

"Here is the spare key for you," said Fortunata, taking it from her bag. "I may not be at home when you come back. I'm guessing you might finish late. Take a taxi. It's cheap here. Do you remember the address?"

Amelia nodded.

"You may stay as long as you like. I'm sure we'll be better off if we stick together."

"Oh, thank you!" Amelia hugged her, and they kissed each other goodbye on the cheeks.

When she returned to the restaurant, Aline, the

hostess, greeted her and led her to a backyard. She said, "Just wait here. Renata will be with you in a bit. She has a visitor."

Two more people were already waiting, a boy and a girl about the same age, and she approached them.

"Hey, I'm Paola! Are you just starting here as well?"

They nodded.

"I'm Viola," said the girl.

"Renan," the boy said, stretching out his hand, which Amelia shook with a smile.

Amelia looked inside through the open door, curtained by a mosquito net. She could see the hallway and the innards of the restaurant.

It was already a quarter past three when the door of the manager's office finally opened.

"I will come back later in case you change your mind. Think well," said a man from behind the door.

"No, thanks. I don't play games of chance," responded Renata's firm voice. "Now, if you'll excuse me, I have people waiting for me."

A middle-aged man with a shaved head left the office, cast a baleful look over his shoulder, and made his way through a dining hall.

"Do you know who that was?" Amelia asked her colleagues in a muffled whisper.

They both shook their heads.

"A bagman?" suggested Renan.

"It's better for us not to know," hissed Viola. "I didn't like the way he looked."

They all nodded.

"Hey, guys. Sorry for making you wait." Renata welcomed them, appearing at the doorstep. "Please, come in."

They went into her office, where she briefly explained the plan for event preparation then sent them to a storage room in the attic and set them to unpacking and untangling electric garlands and decorations. After that, she asked them to rearrange the furniture on the patio.

When they were done, it was already past eleven in the evening, and the restaurant closed for the day. Amelia felt so exhausted after the previous sleepless night and the busy day that her feet were shaking, but the realization that she just finished her first working day and was doing great by herself, despite anything mother said about her ineptitude, filled her with adrenaline.

Renan turned out to be driving and lived not far from Fortunata's place, and Amelia asked him for a ride.

Fortunata wasn't home, but she'd thoughtfully left a pillow and a blanket on a couch. Amelia lay down and immediately fell asleep, tired after the long day.

CHAPTER NINE

WHEN AMELIA WOKE UP AT NINE in the morning, Fortunata was asleep in her bed. She could tell as she heard her groaning and snoring. She was supposed to start her day's shift at the Agave at ten, so she quickly changed her T-shirt, had a glass of water, applied eyeliner to her eyes in a thick line, styled her now-short hair with a couple hand strokes, and went outside to call a taxi.

When she arrived, Renan was already there, eating his breakfast at the patio. They were not getting paid a lot but got a free meal. Amelia went to the kitchen and got her sandwich with bacon and egg and a cup of coffee and joined Renan.

The restaurant was hosting a big event on Christmas Eve, with a samba band playing live music and contests for guests, tickets for which had been sold many months before. They had one last day to finish all the preparations.

Amelia felt agitated at being involved in all this hasty prep work.

"Can't wait to see tomorrow's feast," she told Renan, chewing her sandwich.

"Yeah, it will be cool. And I'm sure we'll get to try all those delicious meals afterward. There's always lots of them left untouched."

"Hey, guys, Renata asked you to clean up on the patio," Aline instructed them. "Come with me. I'll show you where to get inventory."

Viola, who preferred to have her own breakfast at home, had just joined them. They followed the hostess, picked up buckets, mops, brooms, and rags from the storage room, and with them in hand, proceeded to the part of the patio that was normally unused, which was covered in dust.

They spent a couple hours uncovering the furniture, wiping the dust off it, and sweeping and washing the deck. After that, they helped unload a delivery truck and sort out the received goods. Splashing with energy and enthusiasm, Amelia unobtrusively took a leading role on their team. She was hustling back and forth between the kitchen and Aline to ask her approval for each next step.

"All right, guys. Take a break and have lunch. You're doing a great job," said Aline after they sorted out all the perishable goods.

They got their plates of rice with vegetables and

meat gravy from the kitchen and sat at one of the tables they had previously cleaned on the closed patio, as most of the tables were busy.

"Look, it seems like that creepy fella that talked to Renata yesterday is here again," whispered Renan, having looked around the patio after finishing his well-deserved meal.

The girls, sitting with their backs to the space, turned their heads.

"There, see those four guys on our left?" said Renan, looking away from the table he was referring to.

Amelia quickly changed seats, taking one next to him to have a better look.

"Yeah, you're right. It's him," she said, casting a glimpse on the skinhead in a black T-shirt, sipping a beer in the company of similar unfriendly-looking folks covered with multiple tattoos and wearing heavy chains around their necks.

"Renata is not here yet. He's probably waiting for her," suggested Renan.

Amelia bit her lip. "I hope she's not in trouble."

"Anyway, guys, it's none of our business. We are here to help with housekeeping and better stay away from other stuff," Viola reminded them.

They nodded and returned to their food and drinks.

After a break, Aline brought them a tray with kitchen utensils and a huge pile of paper napkins of different colors and showed them how to wrap a napkin around a cutlery set.

"Doesn't seem hard at all," commented Renan. He tried to repeat what she'd done, but the wrap fell apart as he put it on the table.

"Damn!" he spat. "How do you do it, again?"

Aline laughed. "Many hours of practice. Don't worry. You'll learn as well."

She took another set of cutlery and had it artfully wrapped in just a few seconds.

They got to work, and after a few attempts, their results looked passable if not so neat as Aline's example.

"That's funny. I was going to join the army this year but turned out to be unfit for service. Something with blood pressure," Renan shared. "And here I am, practicing origami in a restaurant. You never know where life takes you."

"That's true." Amelia agreed with this philosophical remark.

If only she could tell them of all the things that had happened with her in the past few days...

They finished wrapping the whole tray of cutlery, and Amelia went to the kitchen to drop them off and load another batch.

One of the men who was sitting at the table with Renata's obtrusive visitor took off and followed her.

"Hey, how's it going?" he said. "Sorry, I forgot your name."

"Probably because you never knew it," scoffed Amelia. "I'm new here. Started yesterday."

"Are you sure? I think I met you before."

"Absolutely."

"So do you have a name? I'm Ben, by the way."

"Paola."

"Nice to meet you, Paola. Here, I'll help you." He opened the mosquito curtain on the door for her. "What time do you finish your work?"

"Thanks. I finish late today. Why?"

"We could have a drink together after you're done."

"Thank you, but no. I will need to get some rest before tomorrow's shift."

"Oh, so you work tomorrow as well? I'll drop by, and we can celebrate Christmas Eve together and have a drink. I'm sure your boss will be lax at the time of the feast."

He definitely was hard to get rid of.

"It will be a busy day for us tomorrow. I can't promise anything."

"Don't worry, baby doll. We'll find a way."

He tried to put a hand on her hip, but she dodged. Well, if he was going to be too annoying, she would have to complain to Renata. Or serve him a nice punch in his face. The boss would surely understand.

However, for the time being, Ben retired to the men's room, and she could safely finish her cutlery delivery.

The four gangsta-looking guys stayed at the restaurant for a few more hours, as long as Amelia and her companions were wrapping cutlery, filling napkin dispensers with napkins, and setting the tables in the extended part of the patio for the next day's guests.

Renata came to check their work at about half past

seven.

"You did great today, guys. Thanks a lot," she said. "I want to see you three here tomorrow by six in the morning. We'll start early to have everything ready for the festival. Now, I would like you to go home and get a good rest."

They all confirmed. Renan once again drove the girls to their homes.

As Amelia approached the door of Fortunata's apartment, she heard the sound of conversation and laughter. She knocked, and Fortunata, who looked happy and a bit drunk, opened the door for her.

"Oh, hello, Paola. How was your work today?"

"It was good. We got an early dismissal, for we have to start early in the morning tomorrow."

"That's great. Come in and meet my fiancé, Raul!"

Amelia entered the kitchen and saw a dark-haired man with overgrown bristles on a puffy face, wearing a singlet with a print of a marijuana leaf.

"Raul, dear, it's my new roommate, Paola. Paola from São Paulo." Fortunata grinned.

"Nice to meet you," Amelia told Raul.

He stood up to embrace her and kissed her on her cheek, enveloping her with a smell of chypre cologne, sweat, and alcohol fumes.

"Take a seat, please, and have a drink with us" said Fortunata.

Amelia obediently placed herself on a couch. Plates with cheese, bread, and sliced ham sat on the table with a bowl of vegetable salad, a bottle of wine, and a couple of open aluminum beer cans. Fortunata took a wine glass from the cupboard and poured some wine for her.

"No, thanks," Amelia tried to protest, "I had dinner at the Agave, and I'm not really sure about the drink…"

"Hey, just take a sip to maintain conversation! I just was telling Raul I met someone who appreciated my paintings. How did you put it, again? Postimpressionist something?"

"Why, I also always loved your pictures, honey," objected Raul.

"If only you understood something about them! Paola, she sounds like a real expert. She knows all those smart words."

"Nah, I just really love art and read a couple books about it. I'm not an expert," said Amelia humbly.

"Nati said you moved here from São Paulo. What brought you to this godforsaken place? Why Itajubá?" asked Raul.

"Um, I just browsed the internet and found there were lots of job opportunities here, so I decided to try. I got tired of my mom eating my brain out with a spoon about me not doing anything, so I decided to try my luck here."

"I see you were lucky enough already to meet my Nati. This girl is worth her weight in gold, believe me," said Raul, looking at her with meek puppy-dog eyes. "No one in the whole wide world has such a kind and generous heart like hers."

"Huh, do you hear that?" exclaimed Fortunata derisively. "I wish he were able to come up with such compliments when he's not trying to make an impression on someone else." She feigned slapping him on his face.

Raul seized her by the waist, set her on his lap, and kissed her mouth.

Amelia took a sip from the glass of wine Fortunata had poured her, which tasted quite good, and a bite of cheese and bread.

"Oh, I'm so happy tonight!" Fortunata smiled blissfully. "I don't know about you guys, but I want some music." She took the cavaquinho of the wall and strummed its strings. "Do you know Raul Seixas's 'Gita'?"

Amelia nodded, and Fortunata started singing. Raul and Amelia sang along about the soul-devouring love as well as they could. Amelia felt amazing. Fortunata sang the song with heartfelt passion, and Amelia was sure she could see tears in her eyes.

They sang more songs and drank more wine until it was very late and Amelia delicately told Fortunata that she needed to get some rest before the early-morning shift. Raul and Fortunata retired to the bedroom, and Amelia went to the couch, set her alarm to 5:00 a.m., and immediately fell asleep.

CHAPTER TEN

WHEN THE ALARM WENT OFF, AMELIA took a while to wake up, as she hadn't gotten enough sleep. She got out from under the blanket and looked out the window. The world outside seemed to be sleepy and relaxed at that early hour. Fortunata and Raul were sleeping soundly in the bedroom, so Amelia silently sneaked out of the apartment, called a taxi, and contemplated the weedy yard with blooming azalea bushes while waiting for it to arrive.

At the Agave, everybody seemed to be in a state of full readiness. Renata was giving instructions to cooks, and Aline was discussing something on the phone.

Amelia, Renan, and Viola quickly had their breakfast and started serving tables and decorating the entrance with air balloons. The restaurant was full, and new guests arrived as soon as any tables were free, willing to have a glass of wine or cup of coffee in company of their friends in the middle of late pre-Christmas shopping. The three of them were running head over heels among the regular waiters, taking dirty dishes from the tables to the kitchen and helping to wash them.

They were out of breath by the time the special event started in the afternoon. Amelia and Viola rested for a while in the backyard, having a quick bite, and heard the master of ceremonies shouting something in the microphone while the band played samba.

"Do you have any Christmas plans with your family?" asked Viola. "I feel like I will hardly be able to wake up tomorrow."

"Me too." Amelia wiped sweat off her forehead. "I don't have any family here. I actually just moved to Itajubá."

"Where do you live? Do you rent?"

"I'm staying with a friend currently." Amelia sipped coffee from a paper cup.

"Oh, so you have friends here? That's good!"

"Yeah. It's a bit far from here. It's near the Christian Congregation church and Unicar auto-parts store, but I'm not in a place to be picky."

"I live just a few blocks away. That's why I took this job," admitted Viola. "What's the name of your friend? I know some people in that area."

"Her name is Fortunata. You wouldn't confuse her with anyone. She has curly red hair, and she's a painter. You could've seen her painting somewhere on the street."

Viola knitted her eyebrows. "Fortunata? Fortunata Lima?"

Amelia realized that she didn't know her friend's last name but preferred to nod in affirmation.

"How long have you known her for?"

"Not long, actually…" confessed Amelia, surprised by her coworker's reaction. "I met her a couple days ago when I arrived here and was looking for a place to stay."

Viola sighed. "Oh, you should be more careful choosing friends. Don't you know she's a prostitute?"

Amelia thought about how to answer, sipping coffee in order to pause. Somehow, Viola's words did not seem a shocking revelation, more like something she'd expected to hear. The words of the fat man that had knocked over Fortunata's paintings came to mind.

"She walks the street near the posh hotels and clubs at night and hooks up her clients," blurted Viola with disgust on her face.

"How do you know that?" Amelia asked calmly.

"Everybody in Itajubá knows she's a dirty hooker. If I were you, I would run from her as fast as I can!"

"All right. Thanks for telling me." Amelia took another sip of coffee. "But you know what, I know her as the nicest and kindest person I've ever met, and the fact that she's a prostitute doesn't change that," she said, carefully choosing words.

Viola snorted. "Still, she's a prostitute."

"That makes her a victim, not a villain. It's not about her doing bad things to someone else. It's about other people doing bad things to her, thinking that she can be sold for money like a thing. And she must have gone through something really bad if she's putting up with it."

Amelia thought about Raul and everything Fortunata had said about him and felt a surge of anger.

Viola looked at her in disbelief and disapproval. "It's up to you, but you should really think twice."

They finished their lunch break in silence and returned to work. They carried hundreds more trays laden with plates of delicious festive meals and glasses with drinks of all colors of the rainbow from the kitchen to the tables, then trays of empty plates and glasses back to the kitchen, wiggling their way among the dancing guests.

As the evening descended, the atmosphere became more relaxed. The bartender, Guao, was sneakily handing each of the waiters a portion of mulled wine in a paper cup instead of coffee, when they took their turns for a break.

Amelia took her cup from Guao, who winked at her, and winked back. Drinking warm, spicy wine and breathing the air, filled with the smell of sunburnt glycinia and rhododendron flowers, she wondered what her parents were doing on this Christmas Eve.

She took her phone from her jeans pocket, turned it on, and typed a message: "*Mom, Merry Christmas to you and Dad. I'm safe and sound. Don't worry about me, and be happy on this Holy Night.*" She typed her mother's number, which she knew by heart, in the recipient field and pressed Send.

After a second thought, she composed another

message: "*Merry Christmas. Thanks for your phone. It's indeed very handy.*"

In a minute, an incoming message from the contact named Freak popped up on the screen: "*Merry Christmas, my crazy friend. Hope you are well whenever you are. Better come back soon. Things are getting even more weird here.*"

Amelia smiled and turned the phone off.

By eleven in the evening, the last guests had left, and the restaurant was closing. Amelia, her teammates, and the staff members who were working that night finished the final wrap-up and cleaning in another half hour. Renata paid her temporary helpers their promised reward in cash and dismissed them. Amelia asked Renan to give her a ride again, as calling a taxi on Christmas night would've been futile.

As she entered the apartment, the smell of weed struck her nose, and smoke was floating in the dim light. Fortunata was sitting in the kitchen with a bottle of rum and a cannabis bong.

"Oh. It's you," she muttered, turning her red face, swollen with tears, toward Amelia.

"It's me. Are you all right? This doesn't look like a jolly Christmas dinner." Amelia glanced at the half-empty bottle and the smoking pot.

Fortunata shook her head. "No... Sorry."

Amelia sat on a couch next to her. "What happened?"

"Raul..." Fortunata forced the sound out.

"Of course..." whispered Amelia under her breath.

"What about him?"

Fortunata took another moment to turn her pain into words. "We were going to spend this night together. I cooked dinner and waited for him. He promised to be here by eight. But he didn't come. I called him a million times, but he didn't answer." She stopped, looking forward with empty eyes. "And then one of my friends texted me that she saw him in a bar with a woman."

"I'm so sorry," said Amelia, leaning forward and embracing her.

Fortunata wept out loud. "You don't know what I've done for this man. I went through hell and sold my soul to buy him out of debt and save his life. And he's doing this, again and again, throwing me away like trash for his next whore!"

"Don't let him do it again. He's done enough," said Amelia, pressing her tighter to her chest.

"Why, Paola? How can someone do such things?"

"Well, I guess for the same reason why all bad people do bad things. Because they can and there's no one to stop them." She rhythmically stroked her friend on the back. "But you're the one who must stop him from doing this to you. Just close your door to him and never open it again."

Fortunata just sobbed in response.

"He can only hurt you when you let him into your home and your life," continued Amelia. "It's up to you to draw the line. I know you're hurting now, but let this awful day be the turning point where your new life starts and you no longer put up with such things."

"Yes, you're right... Never again." Fortunata straightened herself, and her gaze seemed less lost as some realization flickered in her eyes. "I paid four thousand reais for his motorcycle repair. I picked it up from the shop today. It's in the basement locker now, and he will not get it back until I get this four thousand back. I wouldn't even be able to count how much I've spent on him in total—I guess it would be enough to buy a house somewhere in the countryside. But this money, I will make him pay. I paid for his stupid motorcycle, and now I don't have money to pay my rent. It's due in ten days... I don't even have money to eat. I spent all that I had left on groceries to make this Christmas dinner—I was so happy to spend it with him..."

Amelia put a hand on Fortunata's shoulder. "Don't worry about it, dear. You have me to get your back, at least with the rent part," she assured her. "Oh, and by the way, I brought lots of yummy meals from the restaurant leftovers." She picked up a fabric shopping bag she'd left on the floor and took out several paper boxes with food. "Here we go. We have fried yams, champagne rice, and three kinds of panettone for the dessert."

Fortunata stood from the couch. "I've cooked Chester chicken, Greek salad, and rabanadas."

"Oh, that's awesome!" said Amelia. "Look, we have a whole feast! And we can freeze some of the food for later 'cause it's too much for two of us, so it won't perish and we'll have meals ready for later. See, life isn't so bad."

A slight smile cracked on Fortunata's face. "Yay, let's celebrate!" She opened the window, and fresh night air streamed inside, clearing out the heavy smell of cannabis smoke and despair.

On Christmas Day, the Agave opened at noon, so Amelia was able to get enough sleep in the morning. That was an easy and relaxed day with not as many guests. The helper team did the final cleanup after the previous night, swept and washed the floors, and changed the decorations that had gotten damaged by the cheering crowd.

She got home by eleven in the evening and found Fortunata painting in the kitchen, her hands and loose black T-shirt covered in multicolored stains.

"Oh, glad to see you in much better spirits today!" Amelia beamed at her.

"What do you think?" Fortunata turned the easel toward her, showing a canvas with the image of a human figure ripping open their rib cage and letting burning flames out of it.

"Oh my goodness! That's really impressive!" Amelia came closer to see it better.

"I just tried to depict what I feel. Don't know if it makes any sense..."

"It does. It's better than any words. I can feel it."

"Thank you, Paola. You know, painting has a healing power for me. When I do it, I feel my anger, fear, and all these bad thoughts burning me inside ceasing, and I feel like I belong to this world and am loved by it and I deserve to walk under the sun and moon, and..." She inhaled fitfully.

"That's so beautiful!" sighed Amelia, deeply moved.

"But when I feel really bad, I don't have the power to start, that initial spark. When I feel like that, drinking is the only thing that keeps me breathing."

"I hope you won't need that anymore." Amelia felt the urge to hug her friend but was afraid of staining her work outfit.

"You're right. I can't do it to myself anymore. I owe myself a better life." She put her brush into a plastic can with paint thinner.

"Absolutely! You are so gifted and special." Amelia's gaze touched the fresh, glossy surface of the painting.

"All right, that's enough for today. I'll remove this mess." Fortunata cupped the paint tubes laid out on the table and placed them into the plastic trunk on the floor. "Are you hungry? I just realized I'm quite hungry. Forgot to have dinner today."

"I had dinner at the Agave, but I would like to have some tea with rabanadas."

"Sure!" Fortunata put the kettle on the stove. "Raul still hasn't called. Not a word from him," she said bitterly while sifting tea leaves in the teapot.

"Ah. Screw him. Good riddance to bad rubbish."

"I still want him to pay me for his motorcycle repair."

"Are there any chances he will ever do it?"

"Darn it, I'll get him to do it," spat Fortunata. "Otherwise, I'll sell his stinky motorcycle."

"Maybe that's what you should do in the first place instead of waiting for him to pay. From what you said, he doesn't seem to be solvent and reliable."

Fortunata pondered that for a moment, wrapping a lock of her ginger curls around a finger.

"Really. Sell the motorcycle if you can find a buyer and send him the money minus that four thousand. It will spare you from seeing his face again." Amelia looked at her friend's perturbed face. "Or if he can give you this money right away and it's a faster and easier option, go that way. I'm just suggesting. It's your decision."

A thought flickered on Fortunata's face, and she headed to her room then returned. "You know what? Take this." She handed Amelia two keys tied together with red twine. "It's a key for the basement and for his cycle. It's better if you have them for now so he can't get them."

"All right. But does he have a key to your door?" asked Amelia warily.

"No… I believe he doesn't. He used to have it, but I made him give it back after our previous fight."

Amelia frowned. "He could have made a duplicate."

"No-o-o. He's far too lazy to bother with that."

Amelia stashed the key in the pocket of her jeans. "Still, I would change the lock."

"Yeah, you're right." Fortunata sighed. "I should think about it."

***

Robert stirred pasta on his plate with a fork, not having eaten it at all, as he sat in the private lounge of an Italian restaurant on Rua Augusta, not far from Procópio Ferreira Theatre.

Lando Lacerdo, who was sitting opposite him, finished his chicken panini, took a sip of water, and leaned back on the soft leather couch. "I appreciate that you found time to meet me, Robert," he said, "I know you're up to your ears in your election campaign."

"You're more than welcome." Robert moved aside the plate and put his hands on the table, his fingers intertwined. "Actually, I was also pretty eager to have a word with you, so I would gladly have come to your office to save you time."

"That's very nice of you to offer, but I'm happy to use this as an occasion to have lunch in the city with such a nice view." Lando glanced through the glass-paned wall. "I can almost never have a normal lunch break at the factory. Somebody always interrupts with some urgent business. But that's what you get for being the one in charge." Lando unfastened a few buttons on his short-sleeved designer linen shirt, took a moist towel from the plate, and wiped sticky sweat from his neck and face.

"I like it here," said Robert. The view over the street below from the height of the fifth floor was rather pleasant, but he was not in the right mood to really contemplate it.

"Nice, eh? Much better than some dim sweltering enclosure they offer you in other diners." Lando lowered his voice. "And what's most important, here we can be sure there's no one eavesdropping around."

Robert nodded. "That's exactly what we need, because—"

"Because everything about this new project is

highly confidential. I know, I know," Lando said. He grabbed his ice water from the table and half emptied it in one gulp.

"Actually, speaking of this project..." Robert started tentatively, "I'm afraid I have to apologize, but—"

"Don't worry about that field trip. I totally understand that you had to delay it. A busy man like you doesn't have enough hours in a day to arrange everything he wants to do. I hear you, my friend."

Robert sighed heavily. "That's what I wanted to say. I think it was a bad idea to kickstart it now. I should put it on hold till all the patent issues are solved, and... and there's just too many things going on that I can't keep under control." He glared at Lando, trying to catch his reaction.

Lando frowned and nodded sympathetically. "There's something really weird going on around this robot harvester."

Robert raised his eyebrows in surprise. "Go on. I'm all ears."

"I did some serious research on this type of equipment and existing patents. There are similar kinds of mechanical coffee harvester, but they are not widely used because they can't sort ripe beans out properly. But it's a problem that calls for a solution, so if your prototype is as good as you say, we can conquer the world with it."

"That's the point I tried to make to you," nodded Robert.

"Yes, I know, I know... So, I considered our production plans for the next year to figure how I can fit the assembly of this harvester into it." Lando drew printouts with diagrams from his suitcase. "Let's say we get several working prototypes ready by the end of February and instantly market them to coffee growers. We could have the first batch produced and dispatched by June, when harvesting begins.

"So I got really enthusiastic about this idea and started to think about which of my engineers and managers I can involve in this project to be sure they don't spill the beans. Of course, they would all sign a strict nondisclosure agreement, but the thing with some people is that they can't keep their mouths shut even if their lives depended on it.

"Thinking about confidentiality led me to the idea of checking my own privacy settings in our corporative network. We have an electronic document-management system designed specifically for our plant—paid a bunch of money for it, but it works perfectly. And there's an option to check who accessed the files you are working with. I'm not much of an IT specialist, but I dig some stuff. And guess what? Somebody accessed the file I created to plan the harvester production."

"Who could it be?"

"That's the weirdest thing. All of the users are registered by their names, but this was some forged account with a random name. I called my system administrator in and asked him, 'What the heck?' He swore he had nothing to do with it. He checked and found out that there was an unsolicited access to my computer from somewhere inside our network, but he couldn't find how it happened." Bruno clasped his hands in indignation.

"Can you trust him?"

"I believe so. Pablo is a good, professional but simple guy, father of three kids, and he's worked with us for over ten years. Not the kind of person who would be involved in some filthy business. Though you never know..."

"Right." Robert frowned. "You never know."

"So, we found out that there's a rat inside the company, digging through my computer, but what's most interesting: they were mostly interested in the harvester because except for these files and a couple more with important financial stats, nothing much was accessed. Pablo and I checked everything."

"Damn." Robert stared intensely at Lando's face and thought he seemed genuinely perturbed. "Any ideas who and why?"

"Holy smokes, Robert, I would pay their weight in gold to someone who could give me any idea. Pablo changed the settings of my network to prevent future access, but I now feel like I can't trust anyone. I copied all the information related to the harvester to my personal laptop, which is not connected to the network, and deleted it from my office computer. Don't know if there's any sense in it. They already got it anyway. I'm sorry, mate. It seems that I let you down," Lando admitted with embarrassment.

Robert raised a palm. "Let's hold off with the penance before we know exactly what happened."

"I invited an independent web-security expert

who's currently working on investigating it, but she honestly said the chances of finding it are close to zero and all we can do is to secure the network from further hacks."

"Sorry to hear about this. It really stinks."

"You're telling me! I don't want to involve the police in it, and I haven't talked about it with anyone except Pablo and told him not to spread it. It's better not to alarm the rat and wait for a further attack. But I know what you're thinking—the most important question is how they knew what to look for. It's like they were after this harvester specifically, while nobody could know that you got me involved in this project..."

They looked at each other with the same doubt in their eyes.

"Nobody except the two of us and Bruno Carvalho," finished Lando.

Robert measured him with a careful look for a moment.

"Don't get me wrong. I don't want to make any accusations." Lando raised a hand as if to guard himself from an obvious remark. "I'm just sounding out the facts."

"Who is in charge of your affiliate Stallion Logistics?" asked Robert.

"Stallion Logistics?" Lando furrowed his eyebrows, trying to remember. "Oh yeah, Ernando Mola, head of the sales department. We don't really do any logistics but registered this unit because of some complicated tax-reduction scheme offered by our accountant. Why are you asking?"

Robert took a folded sheet of paper pressed under his planner cover and showed it to his partner.

"What is this?" Lando looked from the paper to Robert in dismay.

"Vehicle registration record for the Volkswagen van belonging to Stallion Logistics. Can you remember if this cargo van is currently on your balance?"

"Possibly. I'm trying to keep track of everything, but I don't know by heart every unit of equipment Lacerdo Motors has on balance. So, what's with this van?"

Robert looked directly into his eyes. "My daughter, Amelia, almost got kidnapped the night of her graduation party."

"Holy crap! Poor kid—is she all right?"

"Yes. Luckily, she was able to escape. But here's the most wicked part: the vehicle used by the attempted kidnappers belongs to Stallion Logistics. Which, as we clarified, belongs to you."

Lando took in a lungful of air and burst out, "Do you really think that I could do that to your daughter? Who do you think I am? You believe that I could send someone to put a knife to your child's throat and, after that, sit at a table with you like this and eat goddamn panini?" His face turned the ultimate shade of red.

"I'm just sounding out the facts," Robert repeated back to him.

"Well, if you believe that, I don't know what to say to you."

Robert raised his hands in a peaceful gesture. "I don't want to jump to conclusions and make any accusations without proof. That's why I'm here talking to you."

"Well, thank you, I guess." Lando wiped his forehead and took a moment to recompose himself. "As I said, I just revealed there's something rotten in my company that I wasn't aware of. And now you're telling me this news. I swear I will find out the truth and beat the crap out of Ernando Mola if this bastard thinks that he can pull off a scam under my nose and get away with it."

Robert tapped his fingers on the table in consideration. "Can you loop it back to the moment when it all started? When exactly did it happen?"

"The unauthorized access was performed right after I started working on the harvester project, but that means somebody was already preparing for it, boosting malware into our corporation network, waiting for the right moment to attack."

"Have you hired any new employees in key positions recently?"

"That's an obvious question, Robert. Good for you. No. That's the thing—you know my policy—I prefer to promote people who have worked for me for a long time and have proven themselves to be worthy rather than inviting some smarty-pants from outside to put them in charge. Actually, I think I'll hire someone to perform a comprehensive background check on all my managers."

"Well, it's a good policy, I believe, but apparently it's not a panacea. Some of your old employees could be compromised by outsider agents."

"Outsider agents..." echoed Lando. "The question

is 'Who is it?'"

"Are you suspecting Bruno?"

"He's not my obvious rival, but the timing is really suspicious. It happened right after you invited us both to that project. What if he wants to claim the invention? I don't believe in coincidences."

Robert sighed. "Me neither."

"It really stinks that I can't trust anyone. I still need to keep my plant running, and I can't just fire all of them. Or maybe that's what I should do." Lando raised his hands in despair.

"Let's not take any drastic measures for now. What is for sure: we need to freeze the harvester project till things get clear, unfortunately. What we can do in the meanwhile..." Robert rubbed his chin pensively. "I guess we both should take some time to think about it properly before offering any solutions."

***

Later in the evening, Robert and Lucrecia sat in chaise longues on a balcony of their São Paulo apartment, contemplating the sunset, reflecting on the surfaces of surrounding buildings.

"Any results?" asked Lucrecia, opening a bottle of Martini Prosecco and pouring it into two glasses.

Robert rubbed his temples. "Not that I expected much, but everything got even more complicated." He stretched out his legs, clad in home shorts, took a much-needed sip of wine, and recounted his conversation with

Lando to his wife.

"Do you trust him?" asked Lucrecia when he finished.

Robert shrugged. "He sounded earnest."

"Oh, I'm sure he did! If I wanted to ward off suspicion, that's exactly what I would do—come up with a plausible story that would make me look like another victim. That's an obvious solution."

"Is it obvious to you? Sometimes, it scares me to see your mind at work," said Robert half seriously and patted Lucrecia's shoulder, nearly bare and covered only with a strip of her silk pajamas. She smiled a frisky smile and threw her hair to the opposite side, exposing her shoulder even more.

"Yes, you know that you married an evil genius restraining her dangerous trait."

Robert was glad to see her invigorated for the first time in a while. Getting a message from their daughter had seemed to relieve her anxiety.

"But anyway, it's better if he believes that you believed him," resumed Lucrecia. "Even if his cooperation is a mere pretense, there are more chances that he will drop his guard at some point."

"That's what I thought."

"As long as you are being careful what information and levers to give him."

"For sure, I will. If I proclaim myself a politician, I have to be sly and weigh every word." Robert cracked a wry smile and moisturized his mouth with Prosecco. "As for me, I tend to believe him. He's not the kind of guy able to contrive such a complicated plan. He's smart, of course, but too straightforward and uncomplicated for it."

Lucrecia shook her head. "Never judge people by the images they create for themselves. They can be deceptive."

"You're right again. It's so damn complicated that I don't believe we will ever find out the truth. I didn't talk with the inventor team about what happened yet, but I guess I will have to. And I understand that, after that, they might decide to sell their patent somewhere abroad rather than dealing with corrupt Brazilian businesses." He took a big sip from his glass to wash away the taste of this bitter truth.

"Oh... Don't hurry with this, sweetheart." Lucrecia turned to Robert and ran her fingers through his sturdy short-trimmed hair. "I know how important it is for you to have this project launched by Brazilian companies. Believe me, that is no less important to me. I want our country to export something more innovative than coffee and cane. Let's not give up so easily."

"I'm ready to fight to the end, but how?" Robert looked at her pleadingly. "It's hard to fight someone you don't know by sight and can't even see."

"So let's improve our vision."

They sat facing each other in silence for a few minutes, then Lucrecia finally spoke.

"I have an idea on how we can possibly reveal who is behind this. Lando should have a strictly confidential one-on-one conversation with all his key managers and tell them that there's a prospective project for which they're going to need a supplier of electronic modules, and while he considered placing the order with Bruno Carvalho's Digital Era, he has insider information that one of their purchasers is dealing counterfeit electronic components, putting the extra income into their own pocket, and that's why he's wary of dealing with them and needs a substitute. After that, we will see Bruno's reaction. Any signs of massive inspection, dismissals, any fuss... and we will know almost for sure that Bruno has his finger in the pie."

Robert stared at her for a moment. "It's a risky game."

"It is. But it's worth trying. And to find out precisely who Bruno's spy is, Lando could give each of them slightly different information. It would be the best if he knew all the ins and outs of Bruno's company and could name the specific project that was compromised. And we will need to get a real insider into his company to detect the reaction. Some small potatoes, like a secretary or assistant who's aware of what's going on and can be easily greased with an appropriate reward."

Robert furrowed his eyebrows then cracked a thin smile. "It may sound terrible, but I must admit I'm starting to like it. Very intricate."

"You're always welcome." Lucrecia snickered. "And don't feel bad about it. You can't beat those sneaky bastards unless you use their methods."

Robert leaned over and grabbed her in a bear hug. "Senhora del Atore, where would I be without you!"

CHAPTER ELEVEN

THE DAYS BETWEEN CHRISTMAS AND New Year's Day at Agave were filled with multiple blowout parties arranged either by businesses for their employees, or just by groups of friends wanting to celebrate the end of the year, so Amelia and her two teammates were given enough work to keep them on their feet all day long. On New Year's Eve, they had another grand event that went perfectly well.

Renata seemed to be happy with them, except for a mishap when Viola dropped a tray on the floor—luckily, it was just a tray with a few empty dishes, so she just paid their cost and the incident was over—and another time when the boss caught Viola and Renan smoking in front of the building and chastised them for damaging the restaurant's reputation.

Amelia wasn't a smoker and had been lucky enough not to drop anything, so she started fostering a hope that Renata would hire her as a permanent employee after the end of the holiday season. Fortunata and she seemed to be getting along very well, so the search for another place to stay was not on her agenda for the not-too-distant future. She had no idea where her life was going or for how much longer she could live without any documents under her alias, but it was working perfectly for the time being, and she didn't want to worry about anything more than making her living for the next few days, learning the items on the Agave's menu, mastering the art of making small talk with guests, and watching Fortunata slowly recover after her Christmas breakdown. Her artistic friend seemed to create her own little protective bubble of safety, where she enjoyed painting, cooking, and chatting with Amelia during their late-night dinners.

On the second day of January, when Amelia was wiping a vacated table with a cloth and thinking about taking a break in half an hour, she heard a familiar voice behind her.

"Hello, *linda!*"

She turned her head and saw Ben, the tattoo-covered skinhead who'd been hitting on her before Christmas. "I'm not Linda, I'm Paola," she joked without much enthusiasm.

"I know, dear. I just wanted to say that you're beautiful." He put his thumbs in his jeans pockets. "Sorry, I didn't have a chance to come over before—was out of the city—but we can catch up today."

"I have no idea what you're talking about." Amelia measured him with a cold look. "Don't remember that we had any agreement."

"I mean, we should have a drink together," Ben clarified eagerly, moving closer and blocking her way with his wide chest. "I'm free today, and I can pick you up after your shift. This, your Agave, is nice, but I prefer more groovy places."

Amelia stepped backward. "Once again, I don't know where you got the idea that I want to go anywhere with you."

"Why not? I'll buy you a drink and dinner. You are so cute, and I really like you. Why don't you give me a chance?"

Amelia sighed. "Because... I'm not into guys, you know..."

"Say what? Like you're a lesbian?" Ben's eyes bulged.

"Like yes, I'm lesbian."

He took a moment to explore her from top to bottom then concluded, "Nah, you're lying. I don't believe you. Such a pretty gal cannot be a lesbian. They are square and have moustaches. That's because they have all those male hormones."

"I shave my moustaches every morning. That's why you can't see them," explained Amelia earnestly.

"Whatever. I don't care about your moustaches. Give me a chance to make you a proper woman. I'm sure you're after girls just because you haven't been with a real man."

Amelia had to make an effort not to burst into laughter.

"C'mon, try me. It's such a pity that this beauty is just getting wasted, I can't allow it."

She couldn't hold it back. "Ha ha! I see you're a connoisseur of beauty!"

"Exactly! Never heard this word before, but that's what I am! You see, we have a lot to learn and explore about each other."

Amelia rolled her eyes. This squat little man with muscles bunching under his light-brown skin didn't meet her definition of beauty, and neither was he charming or confident, but his persistence was abundant.

"All right, it was nice to chat with you, but my work will not get itself done, so you must excuse me." Amelia raised a hand, waving him away. "I don't want to get in trouble with my boss."

"Sure. I won't hold you up anymore." Ben stepped aside, letting her through. "I'll meet you at eleven when you are closing."

Amelia headed to the kitchen without saying anything.

That night, Renata dismissed them half an hour early, so Amelia left, unaware whether Ben fulfilled his intention to come for her and remembered him only on her way home in a taxi.

She knocked on the door.

"Ah, Paola, come in!" Raul welcomed her. "Nati just made tea. She's waiting for you."

"Hi, Raul. Nice to see you again." Amelia forced

a smile, trying not to give away her astonishment and proceeded to the kitchen.

Fortunata looked so happy that she seemed to be out of this world. Amelia smelled her breath when she gave her a welcoming hug, but she did not seem to be impaired—at least not by alcohol.

"So... you two made up again?" asked Amelia when Raul went to the staircase to have a smoke.

Fortunata beamed. "Yes. Can you imagine? He brought me flowers today!" She nodded toward a bunch of big coral roses in a glass jar on the table. "I would never have expected such romantic moves from him. He never gave me flowers even back when we'd just started dating... And today, he appeared on my doorstep with these beautiful roses and chocolates, and he said that he'd made up his mind and he wants to be with me."

Amelia looked at the flowers with dubious eyes. The image of her friend broken and collapsing in despair not so long before was too fresh in her mind, and she could hardly believe that a bunch of flowers could make up for that.

"Are you sure that you can trust him?"

"We had a good conversation and sorted things out. He said that it's time for him to quit his gambling and start a normal life."

"Well... I'm very glad for you!" Amelia forced a smile. "I hope it works. You are a wonderful person with the gentlest and purest heart, and you deserve a happy and stable life more than anyone."

"Thanks, darling," Fortunata embraced her,

bursting into tears.

"I just want to ask you for something... Don't give him his motorcycle until he pays for its repair."

Fortunata sighed. "I know what you mean... It's hard to say no when my baby is asking me for it, but you're right. I must stand my ground."

"If anything, you can always say that I took it. Technically, it's true."

"I'll just say that it's still in the shop and they won't give it back until I pay. Don't want to involve you in this."

"As you wish, but I want you to know that you can always rely on me. I'm with you, no matter what happens."

The next morning, Amelia left home at eight, as soon as she woke up. She wasn't supposed to start work until ten but preferred to sneak out early and avoid meeting Raul and Fortunata. She told herself it was better to let the reunited couple spend more time alone, but deep inside, she didn't want to see the face of the man who'd wronged her friend so many times and was being given a chance he didn't deserve. She had no experience with situations like this. Maybe her parents were not an ideal pastoral couple—they had their disagreements—but she could never imagine them playing this game of pushing each other on such a roller coaster of extreme emotions. Maybe their relationship style would seem boring to some, but it was less nerve-racking.

Amelia took a taxi to Santiago Square, bought a *pastel de queijo* and a bottle of protein shake in a convenience store, and sat on a bench near the fountains, enjoying the freshness and stillness of the morning hour.

After an hour, when she finished her breakfast and got bored of loitering, she decided to go to the Agave and make some use of her time. She estimated that some of the cooks should be there already and probably Renata, who worked in her office quite early on most days, and she was right. She knocked on the locked front door, and in a minute, Renata opened the door for her.

"Good morning, Paola. You are quite early today!" She looked less like a dashing business lady when she wasn't yet wearing makeup.

"Good morning, senhora. I woke up early today and just wanted to get away from home."

"Same with me. I quite dislike being home lately." Renata sighed. "Since you are here, maybe you could help me with something... Are you good with computers, by any chance?"

"Depending on what you want me to do... I'm not an expert but never had any trouble doing my work in school."

"I'm trying to export a data sheet from my accounting software to an Excel file. Been struggling with it for an hour, to no avail. Maybe you could take a look?"

"Sure. Why not?" agreed Amelia eagerly.

They went to the office, where Renata unlocked her computer and showed Amelia what she was trying to do.

"I never had experience with this software, but exploring the options in Settings is what usually helps."

After several attempts, Amelia demonstrated the desired Excel file saved on the hard drive.

"Awesome! Thank you! I believe I should pay you more today as you saved my day."

"No worries." Amelia smiled. "It wasn't difficult at all. All I would ask for is a big cup of coffee."

"Sure! I'll give you my biggest cup." Renata opened a white cabinet and took a tall mug with Coffee Makes Everything Possible printed on it. "Do you like this one?"

Amelia nodded. "Yes, it's definitely better than the small cups from the bar."

Her eyes caught a framed photograph of a happy-looking couple. The man was hugging the woman, who looked like Renata but younger, and they were both smiling.

"Oh, is this you in this picture?" Amelia asked, taking a closer look.

"Yes, with my husband. He died a year ago." A detectable sadness sounded in Renata's voice.

"Oh, I'm so sorry!" Amelia gasped, regretting her own curiosity. "That... that must be really hard."

"It is..." Renata lowered her head, and her black hair hid her face. "I want to keep this photograph near. It helps me to feel his presence and support. But I don't want to expose it to other people's eyes. That's why I put it in here."

"I understand..." Amelia felt heavy in her heart. "You must have loved him so much."

"I went through fire and water with him... opened the restaurant together. We dreamt about kids, big family, but later, when we would have our business running steady... Like there ever would be a perfect time for it.

Now, it will never happen, and that's what I regret the most."

Amelia wanted to say something but couldn't find any words.

"But the Agave, our restaurant, is our child, and I will not ever surrender it to anyone. Those who killed him will never get their hands on it as long as I'm breathing."

Amelia felt her heart flinch. "Oh my! He was killed?"

"Yes... We disturbed a local gang boss without knowing it, and they started threatening us... Don't want to go into details, but one day, he was found shot outside the city."

"That's so terrible! Did the police find the murderer?"

"No. It was a cold case. But at least the gang was removed from our city, and I did everything I could to make this happen." Notes of metal clung to Renata's voice as she spoke.

Amelia nodded, looking at her with admiration.

"Don't get me wrong, but I accidentally overheard a part of your conversation with that unpleasant man on the first day I started working here," she said after some doubts.

Renata raised an eyebrow.

"The skinhead one with a golden chain. I didn't get much of it, just that he was bugging you really badly. Is he one of those people?"

Renata winced. "Ah. No, he's not. At least, as far as I know. He just imposed some accounting services on me, so to speak." She closed the cabinet as if to show that the conversation was over. "All right. Thank goodness we are alive and well, so let's embrace this day and get our work done. But first, let's go have coffee."

And so they did.

The day's shift was going steadily with its filled tables, the ebb and flow of guests, and the clinking of cutlery being washed in the kitchen, mixed with the rumble of music and conversations.

Amelia was taking a bottle of liquid soap to refill the dispenser in the washroom as Aline had asked when she heard a familiar voice talking by the phone behind the door. Ben was there again.

CHAPTER TWELVE

AMELIA OVERCAME HER INITIAL URGE to flee as far as possible and tried to hear his conversation.

"No, we have everything settled already. Tomorrow at seven p.m. at our base in Lindageral. Bring all the lot right here and don't get in any trouble on your way. I'll meet you there, and be sure I'll count everything," he said, raising his voice in indignation.

Amelia felt a sudden jolt of adrenaline. A base in Lindageral? What business did this suspicious man have in her hometown? As Ben finished his phone call, she quickly retreated to the storage room next door to avoid meeting him. The time was already past nine p.m., and Ben seemed very likely to be there to get her attention again. She heard his steps as he exited the washroom and waited for several minutes before coming out.

Viola was passing by and nearly got hit by the door. "What have you been doing there?" she asked, giving her a wary look.

"I was just getting soap. Need to add some to the washroom." Amelia raised the bottle.

Viola pursed her lips. "There's some guy asking for you," she said with obvious disapproval on her face.

"Really?" Amelia raised her eyebrows. "Who could that be?"

"You know better. The one with the shaved head and skulls tattooed on his arms."

"Doesn't sound like any of my friends."

"I'm sure you have a lot of them," Viola scoffed and proceeded to the kitchen.

After she'd heard that Amelia was staying at Fortunata's place, she got demonstratively cold and snooty with her, not missing any chance to pick on her. That was both frustrating and amusing for Amelia, but she preferred to ignore it, acting as friendly with her as always—and even more, sometimes in an exaggerated way. Conflict was the last thing she wanted.

Amelia quickly refilled the washroom soap dispenser and headed to the restaurant hall, where Ben was sitting at the bar with a mug of beer. He made eye contact with her and expressively raised his beetling eyebrows.

"Hey, pretty, how's life?"

"Pretty good, thanks."

"I was here that night to pick you up, but you

bailed on me.”

“Oh, did I? I guess I just got tired by the end of the day and didn’t remember what you said.”

“Well, today I have plenty of time, and I’m not going anywhere without you.”

Amelia sighed. She could’ve asked the bartender to kick him out or call the police, but his excessive attention looked like an opportunity to find out what connected him to Lindageral.

“All right. Another hour and a half, and I’m free.”

“Sounds good!” Ben smirked.

Amelia cleaned up a couple of tables, thinking intensely about what Ben might be up to and what she could possibly do to find it out. She asked Aline to dismiss her for a short break and went outside through the front door, where she took her cell phone out and turned it on. She walked across the street while it was booting up to ensure no one in the Agave would overhear her conversation. The street was empty and already dark. Amelia dialed the number saved under the name Freak. She waited impatiently for what felt like an eternity, listening to the long, annoying beeps.

“Hello?” Marcelu sounded surprised.

“Hey there, Mr. Great Detective. I have something to tell you very quickly. Are you alone now?”

“One second…” Something rumbled in the distance. “Yes, I’m out in my backyard now. What happened?”

“So, long story short. I ran into one very creepy fella who’s planning some suspicious business in Lindageral tomorrow. I’m almost sure he’s involved in some criminal gang."

"Oh!"

"Yes, exactly, oh. I overheard him talking on the phone, and he's going to meet someone at seven p.m. at their base in Lindageral. I will try to fish any other information from him, but your work in the meanwhile is to think about where their base could possibly be."

"That's... quite a task," said Marcelu after a pause.

"Think hard. You know our town. You've crisscrossed it all on your bike and explored every corner. Think about it... If you were a gangster looking for a place to gather with your sidekicks, what place would you choose for your base?"

"Well... I guess somewhere out of sight. On the outskirts, where there are not many houses around."

"See, that's already something to start with. Now think which of the outskirts fit better for it."

"Okay, I will," promised Marcelu.

"That's my boy. All right, I got to go back to work now."

"Wait! What are you going to do about that gangsta guy?" he interrupted her nervously. "Please tell me you are not going to get in any trouble. It's not worth it at all. Better come back here and report everything you have observed to my dad, and let the police handle it."

"All right, all right. I'm not some stupid little girl. I can take care of myself," grumbled Amelia, heading back toward the Agave.

Marcelu sighed. "Fine. I hope you know what to do. But please, don't play superhero!"

"I know. I'll be careful. Do your part, now. Talk later." She hung up and went inside the restaurant, noticing Ben playing on the slot machine in the corner of the lounge.

Renata dismissed her early, half an hour before the restaurant closed. Amelia took off her apron, left it in the storage room, and waved at Ben. He followed her to the exit.

"Shall we go?" he asked.

"Where do you want to go?"

"There's a bar near the marketplace. I'll drive us there."

"Um... no, I don't think so." Amelia shook her head. "You've been drinking. It's a bad idea to drive now."

"It was nonalcoholic beer!" blurted Ben.

"Doesn't matter. You'll be drinking in the bar, I assume. I have a better idea. There's a pub just two blocks away. We can take a walk."

"If you wish," he agreed reluctantly.

They passed Santiago Square and the Universal Church and ended up at an unprepossessing building with a sign reading Bar de Coluna. It was a cramped place with wooden benches and loud house music playing from speakers.

"What do you want to drink?" asked Ben.

"Herbal tea."

He laughed. "You're funny. You don't go to a bar to drink tea."

"Why? There is no such rule."

"Have a glass of wine, at least. You need to relax

after work." He turned to a waiter, a skinny young boy who approached them. "Whiskey with cola for me and a glass of wine for my girl," he commanded.

"What kind of wine? We have a list of twelve."

"Any of them." Amelia waved her hand. "Something light."

The boy nodded and, in five minutes, returned with glasses. Ben took his highball with brown liquid and took a big gulp.

"So how is work in the Agave? Any fun there?" he asked.

Amelia nodded. "Lots of fun."

"Is your boss nice to you? I heard she can be quite a bitch. Let me know if she doesn't treat you well, and I'll have a talk with her."

"Where did you hear that from?" Amelia knitted her eyebrows. "Actually, she is the nicest person you could possibly have as your boss. She can be strict sometimes, but that's just what her job takes."

Ben laughed. "I see you are a good girl. A diligent one. I like it." He looked at her contentedly.

"Pff... I'm good as long as nobody pisses me off. When that happens, I can be very bad."

"Oooh, that would be interesting to see. I bet you're a hot thing as well." Ben grinned even wider.

"What about you? What are you doing for work?"

"Just hustling here and there."

"What would that mean?" asked Amelia apprehensively.

"I'm kind of a logistics manager. Too long to

explain. Don't want to talk about work now." He took another mouthful of his glass.

"Have you lived here in Itajubá all your life?" Amelia continued questioning.

"Nope. Actually, I don't even live here. It's hard to tell where I live. I'm always on the road. Since I was dismissed from the army, I haven't spent more than a week in one place."

"So you served in the army?"

"Five years. It was a good school of life. Made me who I am. I never knew my parents, was raised in a Catholic orphanage."

"Oh, sorry to hear! It must have been tough."

"Yep, was pretty shitty. Army was much better." He drained his glass and put it on the table with a bang. "So, how do you have fun when you don't work?"

Amelia shrugged. "Um... Lots of ways. Sing songs with my friends, go to the beach, smoke pot." The wine and adrenaline boosted her imagination, and she decided to get into character.

"That's cool. We should do it someday together."

"What exactly?"

"Everything." Ben smirked.

At that moment, his phone rang. He swore under his breath, scooted away from the table, and went outside.

Amelia took her cell phone and hastily typed a message to Marcelu: "I have an idea. I need you to trace my phone location. Can you do it?"

His response followed immediately: "Are you okay???"

"Yes, just do it, details later."

"Sure. One sec."

In a minute, she received a message from the mobile provider requesting her permission for tracking and confirmed it. She sent another message, that time to Renata: "I need a day off tomorrow, family issues."

After that, she activated the call-redirection service, referring all incoming calls to Marcelu's number, and put the phone in silent mode.

"Problems?" she asked Ben when he sat back at the table.

"Nope. Just work stuff." Nothing remained of his previous relaxed contentment. His face was so rigid and harsh that Amelia felt uncomfortable.

"At this hour?"

"Yep. It happens sometimes. Had to take care of something." His black eyes looked at her intensely. "Do you want another drink?" He glanced at her unfinished glass of wine.

"No, I'm fine. It's a bit sweltering in here. I'm feeling dizzy. Let's go outside."

"Sure, sweetie. As you wish." He paid the bill at the counter, and off they went into the darkness of the night.

As the Bar de Coluna door closed behind them, Ben turned his body toward Amelia, seized her by the shoulders, and pressed his lips against hers before she realized what was happening. Nobody had ever kissed her that way, and though it was absolutely inappropriate and insolent, her curiosity prevailed over her indignation, and she succumbed to his impetuous move and put her hands around his tight muscular body. His arms holding her were very warm, his bronze skin seeming to radiate heat. Amelia felt an electric current running through her body. A sense of danger struggled with the sensual pleasure of feeling the body of this sketchy stranger pressed against hers.

Ben let go of her and laughed. "Damn. Lesbian girls are good kissers!"

"You betcha!" She smirked nonchalantly.

"Let's go to my car." Ben put an arm around her waist and nudged her to move.

Amelia felt her heart pounding heavily in her chest as they walked in silence through the pitch-black night. The picture of what she was going to do was very clear in her head. It was plain and simple, and she desperately hoped that nothing would go wrong.

Across the street from the Agave, they approached a black Toyota Corolla. Amelia read the license plate— LBM 9418—and tried to memorize it.

Ben unlocked the car and opened the passenger door for her. "Here you go."

They both climbed in.

"What kind of music do you like?" asked Ben, turning the radio on.

"Many kinds. Rock, tropicana, samba."

While he clicked the button trying to find the right frequency, Amelia sneaked the phone from her pocket and tucked it under the rubber mat beneath her seat.

"I guess Transcontinental FM will do." He finally picked up reception for a radio station playing popular music.

"Yeah, it's good," agreed Amelia. Ben leaned toward her and kissed her, lifting her shirt while Renato da Rocinha sang about his life's philosophy in his hit "Castelo de Um Quarto Só."

"Wait, what are you doing?" blurted Amelia when she finally overcame her jitters.

"What's wrong?" Ben looked at her with blurred eyes.

"What the hell do you think you're doing?" she shouted. "I thought we were only going for a ride! You think that if I went out with you, I'm ready for anything?"

"Hey, hey, cool down! I didn't mean to piss you off."

"I'm out of here!" Amelia snapped the door open and bolted out.

"Hey, let me at least drive you home! Paola!"

"No way! I don't trust you! I knew all men were jerks!" Amelia yelled at the top of her lungs, putting as much expression in her voice as she could. She'd never lashed out at anyone in her life for real, so she had to lean into the role. She imagined what Fortunata would do.

"What's wrong with you? I didn't do anything to you, you psycho!"

"Don't you dare follow me, or I'll scream so much that all the city will hear it!" Amelia wasn't inclined to find out if anyone would hear her and react, so she took off running through the dark square.

After five minutes, when she ended up on one of the narrow streets on the other side of Teodomiro Santiago

Square, she stopped to catch her breath and made sure that Ben wasn't following her. Everything around her was empty and silent. Worried that he might circle around the streets, trying to find her, she took a shortcut through the back streets and walked at a fast pace till she found herself in front of the Embaixador Hotel. A taxi was dropping off a passenger, and she sprinted toward it, waving. Luckily for her, the driver noticed her and stopped.

Amelia flopped onto the backseat, fastened her belt, told the address to the driver, and finally exhaled in relief. She'd completed her mission with success—at least the first stage of it. She relished her small victory, looking at the dim lights of the city, flickering outside the moving car.

The time was already past one in the morning, so Amelia opened the door with her key, trying to not make any noise. But as soon as she entered the apartment, she realized she had no reason to be quiet. The light in the kitchen was on, and Fortunata was awake, sitting in the kitchen with her knees pressed to her chest. The second thing she noticed was a huge mess of shoes, clothes, and toiletry from the dresser, lying on the floor near the knocked-over shoe rack.

Amelia approached Fortunata. "What happened here?"

She lifted her head, and Amelia noticed a bruise on her cheekbone.

"Did you have a fight with Raul?"

Fortunata nodded.

Amelia kneeled on the floor next to her. "I'm so

sorry, Nati." She delicately stroked her shoulder.

"You were right. I shouldn't have trusted him. It was all just a game. All this—flowers, apologies, promises. Just a goddamn game." She stuck her face in her knees and sobbed. "He just wanted to get his motorcycle back. When he asked me and I told him to pay me for the repair first, he started shouting at me. Called me a dirty whore. Like it wasn't him who'd made me one."

"Please, calm down. I can imagine how it hurts, but this was absolutely predictable. He will never change. You have to remove him from your life, or he will ruin it."

"Yeah, I know. I couldn't stand his insults and punched him in the face, and he punched me back. But I also left a few marks on his face." She smirked, touching her bruise.

"Please, don't let him do this to you anymore. I guess there's no way he'll leave you alone voluntarily. Let's hit the road and go somewhere far from here, together."

Fortunata smiled. "I like this idea!"

"Why not? Let's take your cavaquinho and shakers. We will travel by hitchhiking from town to town and earn money playing and dancing in squares. What do you think? Would that make enough to keep us fed? I think it could."

"Yeah, it would be a better life than rotting in this city." Fortunata leaned toward Amelia and hugged her. "I'm so lucky I have you by my side. You are my guardian angel, Paola!"

"And I will guard you," promised Amelia. "I hate it when good and innocent people suffer. Now, let's go to bed. It's very late."

"Sorry. You must be tired. I guess I'm not a very good roommate, with all these feuds," sighed Fortunata.

"Don't worry about me. You need to take care of yourself first of all. Though I must admit I had a very long and tiring day, and I'm barely standing on my feet."

Amelia poured herself a glass of cold water from the kettle.

"Can you lie with me?" asked Fortunata. "I'm so scared to be alone."

As they lay side by side on the bed, Amelia said, "You know, I got kissed by a boy today for the first time in my life."

"No way! How was it? Who is he?"

"I met him in the restaurant. It was fun, but not as I imagined it. Not like they show in movies, like you soar up in the clouds. It was very... physical."

"Oh, it depends on who you are kissing." Fortunata smiled. "But seriously, first time?"

"Yes. I've never dated anyone. When I was fifteen, there was one boy, my girlfriend's brother... I really liked him. He was older than me and very cool and fun. I tried to get his attention all the time. He studied philosophy at university. I started to study it also, to show off for him. Asked him to lend me his books. He liked existential philosophy the most and criticized Friedrich Nieztsche. He was surprised when I asked but gladly gave them to me and then asked my opinion."

"I spent days reading, and my parents started getting worried that I was having some kind of crisis.

They couldn't understand why I'd gotten so obsessed with finding the meaning of life all of a sudden."

"Like they were concerned that you were reading too much? Well, that's funny."

Amelia chuckled. "Yeah, exactly! I guess parents of teenagers are normally worried about finding illegal stuff in their room or them spending nights away from home. But can you imagine parents that want to have a serious conversation with their daughter after finding books of philosophy in her bedroom?"

"It seems like you've found a different way to freak out your family."

They both laughed.

"So I had to explain that I was not being depressive, just influenced by Noel's enthusiasm about philosophy. Of course, I didn't say directly that I was trying to impress him, but I suspect they guessed. My dad said I was way too robust and wholesome, and it would take a lot of German philosophers to do any damage to my sanity." Amelia giggled again. "I even got hurt a little bit that my dad didn't think I was a complicated and sensitive soul."

"And what about that guy?"

"Oh, I didn't miss any chance to go to my friend's house and meet her brother. She knew, of course, what was going on and was very supportive. We would talk with him for hours. He liked to discuss his favorites, Arthur Schopenhauer and Immanuel Kant, and was admired that I was able to perceive them. It was a challenge for me, and I was up to it. And it seemed like I was successful. I was up in the clouds. He was all I could think about.

I daydreamt of us traveling around the world together...
Just to find out very soon that he'd started dating a girl
from his university..."

"Aw, crap!"

"Yeah. I should have known from the beginning
that I was just his sister's funny little friend. I felt so
broken I could barely eat for three days, and I pretended
to be sick, to not go to school. But at least he left me well-
read in philosophy." Amelia laughed sardonically. "I guess
we wouldn't be happy together anyway. He doesn't like to
travel. He hardly goes anywhere far from his computer
and books."

She looked at Fortunata, who seemed to be
half asleep, and closed her eyes, and in a moment, her
exhausted mind switched itself off.

CHAPTER THIRTEEN

WHEN AMELIA WOKE UP, FORTUNATA was already up and cooking breakfast in the kitchen.

"Good morning," Amelia said. "Oh, you're making pancakes!"

Dishevelled Fortunata gave her a weak smile. "Yeah, I woke up an hour ago and had to get myself doing something to stop thinking."

"I was wondering—did you ever try to sell your paintings online?" asked Amelia when they sat at the table to eat pancakes with strawberry jam and drink coffee. "There are lots of platforms on the internet where you can do it. You can auction them off and maybe even get some decent money."

"Never thought of it," admitted Fortunata.

"Sometimes, I manage to sell one or two, standing on the street, but it doesn't happen very often. You should teach me how to sell online."

"For sure. I believe you deserve acknowledgement. I've seen paintings much worse than yours getting sold for outrageous prices. I think you may need a computer, but you can start just using a smartphone."

"By the way, I want to go to the Marketplace now. It turns out I lost my phone somewhere yesterday, and I need to buy a new one. I can also check if there are some cheap preowned laptops. Or maybe you would like to go with me?"

"Nah, I need to clean up all this mess, and I'm feeling a bit dizzy after yesterday's fighting. If you find a good deal, let me know."

When Amelia went outside to the taxi waiting for her, her thoughts switched to urgent operation mode. Ben was somewhere out there, an alleged gangster up to something malevolent, with her phone in his car as a tracking device, which he hopefully hadn't noticed, and he supposedly had an appointment with his partner in crime somewhere in Lindageral in less than twelve hours.

At least Marcelu was tracking him, and he was smart enough to react appropriately even without any further contribution from her, but she didn't feel like staying to one side anymore.

Amelia found a store selling refurbished digital devices and bought a preowned smartphone for 130 reais, making sure that it was fully functional and had a good enough camera, and asked for a prepaid phone card with mobile data.

Overwhelmed with anticipation, she hurtled out of the Marketplace and headed towards Sapucaí River to find some privacy, where she turned under the bridge toward a grassy slope. Amelia took a look around to ensure nobody could overhear her then pounded Marcelu's number into her new phone and dialed it.

"Hi, it's me," she said.

"Oh, thank God. I was so worried! Can you finally explain what's going on?" Marcelu burst out. "I tracked your phone all night. The signal went from Itajubá to Brasopolis. What are you doing there?"

"Hey, calm down. First of all, I'm fine. I stashed my phone in that guy's car, so what you're tracking now is his itinerary."

"Oh great! I didn't sleep the whole night, tracking the signal and wondering what it was supposed to mean."

"Marcelinho, I'm so, so sorry! Believe me, I wouldn't bother you if I wasn't sure it was important," pleaded Amelia. "I also had a rough night, if it makes you feel better. I got myself groped all over just so we could set up this tracker."

"What? Are you serious? How is that supposed to make me feel better?" Marcelu yelled. "Where are you now? I need you to come back here. You don't know what you are dealing with."

"I'm in Itajubá. You're right. I think it's time for me to come back. It will be more effective if we cooperate. I'll be there tomorrow if not today."

"Finally."

"Please, keep track of Ben. His estimated arrival time at 'the Base' is seven p.m. today. That's when we'll know its location for sure, if everything goes right. This is my new number I'm calling you from. Could you set up its tracking as well, just in case?"

"Be sure I'll not let you off the radar, you lost girl!"

"One more thing. Write down his license plate number: LBM nine four one eight, and try to find out everything you can about him in the meanwhile. Just to keep you busy and prevent you from freaking out."

"You're freaking efficient at this, you know."

Amelia chuckled. "Hope to see you soon."

She strolled back to the Marketplace and took one of the taxis waiting at the curbside to make a quick trip to Fortunata's place to pick up her backpack and give her money for the rent, and then immediately head to Lindageral. She felt somewhat uneasy leaving her friend at the peak of her personal crisis, but her urge to investigate the alarming activity happening in her hometown prevailed at the moment, so she promised herself she would get back to Fortunata later.

As soon as Amelia opened the lobby door, she heard a man shouting something, his angry voice resonating in the stairwell. In a moment, she recognized the voice. It was Raul. Instantly, she bristled and went up the stairs, treading softly. She stopped two flights of stairs below Fortunata's apartment on the uppermost, fourth floor, turned on the camera on her phone, and started filming a video.

"You think you will get away with it, you bitch?"

yelled Raul. "You will give me back my Ducati, or you'll regret it!"

Behind the door, the woman answered something Amelia couldn't hear.

"Open now, I said!" He pounded on the door with all his might. "You can't just hide inside all the time like a rat. I will get you anyway! I will beat the shit out of you! I'll make you choke on your own blood, you whore! Can't you hear me?"

Another volley of fierce pounding.

"What do you think of yourself? You are nobody, a street hooker! I'll smash your face and make sure no one ever will want your services even if you pay them!"

Amelia pressed the button to save the video and silently retreated down the stairs and outside, considering her options. Fortunata was safe for a while behind the locked door—she hoped it was durable enough—but she was very unlikely to call the police. No, she would be too afraid to get in trouble with them even if her life was at stake. But her life *was* at stake. Raul didn't look like he was joking.

Amelia dialed 190 and reported that a violent man was threatening her and her roommate and they were afraid to go outside. After that, she went across the yard to keep an eye on the entryway and stay unseen, in case Raul came out and sat on the grass. While she was observing the scene, she went to the police of Itajubá's web portal to the Report a Crime section and uploaded the video proof followed by a detailed description of what had happened, hoping that would induce a reaction even if Fortunata preferred to make no statement.

The state of things was far beyond what was acceptable for noninterference.

She looked at the phone screen again and again, tracking the time that passed. Fifteen minutes... twenty-five... half an hour. Nothing seemed to happen. The police seemed to not be in a hurry, and Raul was still there. What if...?

Amelia jumped to her feet and rushed toward the entrance. She ran up to the fourth floor without stopping. Fortunata's door was closed, and Raul was not there. She leaned her head against the door and listened closely. She heard a muffled rumble of voices talking about something in a low-key tone.

After a sigh of relief, she felt annoyance about Fortunata opening the door to the aggressive man. Well, as strange as it was, at least she was safe for the moment. Fortunata seemed to have talked him into something, at least for the time being.

For the lack of a better idea, Amelia went one floor down, sat on the stairs, and went into standby mode. In another twenty minutes, she heard footsteps on the stairs and was happy to finally see uniformed men heading toward Fortunata's apartment. She stepped aside, letting them go.

"It's here, number twenty-four," one of them said and knocked on the door. "Good afternoon, senhora. We got a call from you, saying that you are being threatened."

Amelia couldn't distinguish Fortunata's response, but she heard Raul shouting.

"What, you called the cops, you lying whore?"

She also heard the noise of what sounded like a fight. She stirred herself from her stupor and hurtled down the stairs and behind the corner of the building. In a while, she saw two policemen leading Raul, handcuffed, out of the entryway and making him sit in the backseat of their car. Then she could finally exhale.

Amelia took a couple minutes to recompose herself and went to the apartment. Fortunata's bruise-ornamented face was pale and disturbed when she opened the door.

"Raul just got arrested," she said. "Some of the neighbors must have called the police."

"It was me. I heard him threatening you, and I had no choice," confessed Amelia, looking straight into her desperate brown eyes, which became fierce with indignation as soon as the words reached her mind.

"What? Why? Who asked you to do that?"

"Hey, what was I supposed to do? Fight with him? Let him kill you? It didn't sound like he was joking, not at all!"

Fortunata groaned and slapped herself on the forehead. "He was simply drunk and blurting rubbish, like... Well, you know how it happens!"

"No, I have no idea. And it doesn't justify him in any way." Amelia tried to make eye contact with her friend, who seemed to be beside herself in frustration.

"Now, I have to get him out of jail! He disobeyed the cops and is in serious trouble."

"Oh, I hope he is! I filmed a video of him shouting

and threatening you and uploaded it to the police website. Now they have proof.”

Fortunata looked at her in disbelief for a moment then screamed at the top of her lungs, “What the hell have you done, you bitch? Do you even realize? After all this, he will never be with me—never! He will go to that slut Hideko now. I’m sure she will bail him out!” She clenched her fists and wailed.

“For goodness’s sake! Can you just calm down?” Amelia tried to put a hand on her shoulder.

She shrank back. “You want him for yourself. That’s why you’re interfering? He would never even look at a tomboy like you.”

“What are you talking about? He’s not good at all, not good for anyone. I don’t want any girl to be with him because he’s a psychopath!”

Fortunata howled aloud like a wounded dog and smashed a plate that sat on the counter, onto the floor.

“Nati, I’m so sorry, but you don’t see the obvious truth. You would never have anything good with him.”

“How dare you? You’re just jealous. You’re jealous because no man ever looked at you and never will! You’re a laughingstock! You don’t even look like a woman!”

“Well, I’m only happy if Raul and blocks like him aren’t looking at me. Look what he has done to you! He’s only messed up your mind and screwed up you and your life. You can’t continue a life like this. It will destroy you!”

“Shut up, you bitch! You think you’re better than me? Is your life any better?”

“No, no. Fortunata, wait! You don’t understand!”

Amelia stretched out her arms toward her helplessly. "I didn't mean to judge you. All I want is to help. I am your friend."

"Friend! All you did is ruin my life. I wish you'd never crossed my path. Get out of my place!"

"For sure, that's what I'm going to do!" Amelia grabbed her backpack from behind the couch and made her way out before the situation got completely out of control.

She rushed down the stairs and stopped in the entryway, frantically thinking what to do next. She had to get to Lindageral, and she had to admit that she couldn't wait to meet Marcelu—what a pleasure it would be to talk to someone sane and reasonable at last!

Amelia considered hitchhiking all the way, then a desperate thought crossed her mind. She stuck her hand in her banana bag and touched the basement key Fortunata had given her. Taking the motorcycle without permission would be a highly questionable move, especially after their fight, but at the same time, it was a much more reliable way to get to her destination.

She promised herself she would return it to Fortunata later or cover its cost, and she headed to the storage room in the basement. It was dark and dusty, and Amelia turned on her phone's screen to be able to see. Some old furniture sat there, along with wooden boxes and bicycles, and she finally saw an orange Ducati motorcycle.

Amelia didn't have any type of driver's license, but one of her older friends from São Paulo had taught her how to ride a motorcycle, and that one didn't look challenging at all, so she climbed onto it and turned the key. The motorcycle roared and blasted off.

The fuel level was close to empty, so she pulled over at the nearest gas station to top off the tank and buy a big bottle of water. Another problem was that she had no helmet, and besides just being dangerous, that could draw the attention of potential road patrols on her way. And that was the last thing she wanted, considering that she would be riding without a license. So she used the map in her phone to find the nearest car-and-motorcycle-parts store, just five minutes away, and dropped in to get a helmet with a face shield.

With the helmet on her head, Amelia felt like an armored knight. The black-tinted shield fully hid her face, which brought her more confidence. She put her route to Lindageral into her phone's navigator and turned on voice directions.

Driving on the busy highway was incredibly scary at first. Amelia clenched her hands on the steering bars in a white-knuckled grip and maneuvered her way to the left lane. Once she adjusted to the traffic, she found it wasn't bad at all. The rhythmic roar of the engine and the road signs flickering by released her sense of freedom and speed. She understood Raul's obsession with his motorcycle—the little beast sped up easily in a few seconds and ran steadily.

Before she knew it, Amelia exited Itajubá. She turned left at the fork to the Santo Antônio Bridge, crossing the narrow but determined Sapucaí River, whose brown waters ran far to the north to merge with Rio Grande. Meanwhile, Amelia made her way south, down the road looping between green hills, pastures, farms, and small towns. Luckily for her, the traffic wasn't heavy, and she felt so charmed by the serenity of the landscape surrounding her and the tamed power of the motorcycle beneath her that she was surprised to find herself entering Lorena, in the state of São Paulo, which meant she'd completed most of her trip and was half an hour from Lindageral.

The sky was clear blue, save for scarce light clouds, and though the time was already past six in the evening, the sun was blazing ruthlessly. The helmet with the tinted screen protected her face and head from its rays, but at the same time, it made her sweat underneath. Seeing a roadside cafe, Amelia decided to make a stop. She left her motorcycle near the entrance so that she could see it through the window. After taking off her helmet, she wiped her face, covered with small beads of sweat, using a paper napkin she grabbed from one of the tables.

"One cola with ice, please," she asked the middle-aged woman working there, who looked at her askance.

Amelia sat at a table by the window and took a sip of the refreshingly cold drink. She had to use another napkin to dry her phone, which had gotten moist with sweat in her jeans pocket. She'd missed three calls from Marcelu, so she called him back.

"Where are you?" he blurted impatiently without any greeting.

"I'm on my way. In Lorena at the moment. I had to

deal with some unexpected trouble, so it took longer than I expected. Got any news?”

“I’m tracking your guy, and he’s approaching Lindageral now. He passed by Guaratingueta about fifteen minutes ago.”

“Excellent! The bird is flying directly to the cage!” yelped Amelia in rapture.

“Yep, if your suspicions are true, we will know the epicenter of their activity and can arrange surveillance.”

“It would be cool to find out what they are up to today...”

“Well, yes, but first of all, let’s not act in a rush, or we might just spook them. We don’t know the location, so it will take time to prepare and explore the whereabouts to find an observation point. And if you are right about them, we could put ourselves in danger by going in unprepared.”

“Makes sense,” agreed Amelia.

“When are you arriving? Do you want to come over so we can discuss everything? Or you want to go home first?”

“Um... I’m not sure I want to go home. If my parents are home, there for sure will be a huge scandal, and I’m not ready for that today. I think I’ll just ask Charlotta or another of my friends if I can stay at their place for a night or two and then decide what to do.”

“You can stay at my place!” suggested Marcelu eagerly.

“Oh... Thanks a lot, but that might be not the best idea, considering that our dads are bosom friends. Don’t want to tamper with their relationship. I'm feeling like I'm tiptoeing among water balloons that are ready to explode and flood everything around. That's why I prefer to just disappear."

Marcelu sighed. "Right. Do as you will. I'm not pushing you."

"I appreciate it. I'll be in Lindageral in about half an hour. By that time, you should already know the coordinates. Send them to me as soon as you get them. I'll ring you when I arrive."

"Aye, aye, Captain!"

Amelia finished her drink, used the washroom, washed her face with cold water, and put the helmet back on her head as she went to the stolen motorcycle to continue her trip.

CHAPTER FOURTEEN

THE SUN STARTED TO SET, AND THE HEAT subsided, so the last leg of her journey went smoothly. Amelia felt agitation rising in her chest as she passed the sign saying Welcome to Lindageral! After searching for a place to make a quick stop without drawing attention, she turned to a parking lot near the local hospital. She parked the motorcycle at a rack, sat on a bench nearby, and took out her phone. The time was already 7:20, and three messages had come in from Marcelu: a link with geographical coordinates at 7:00, then *"He left the spot and is driving out of town to the southwest"* at 7:18, and finally *"Where are you???"* a minute before.

Amelia groaned in indignation. Ben was gone, and she was late. She had no clear plan but had hoped she would be able to see whoever he was meeting with. For some reason, she'd expected this to shed some light on what was going on. She put the phone back in her pocket, closed her eyes, and lowered her head to her folded hands.

After taking a moment to calm down and reflect, she opened the message with the link and clicked on it. Her navigation app showed her the point on the map, which was on the west side of town, near a building that looked like a secluded farm. It was just a few kilometers away from her parents' estate but located on another road.

Amelia requested the navigator to show her the shortest way to get to the point and mounted the orange Ducati again. She passed by the house, which looked like it had been uninhabited for a long time and was now under renovation. Grass had taken root on the roof. Piles of bricks and steel sheets were stacked in front of the house, covered with plastic film. She headed down the road far enough not to be noticed from the farm, if anyone was there to watch. A small grove divided the dilapidated household from a vast coffee plantation. Amelia passed by the grove then dismounted and turned back toward the mass of Brazilian pepper trees. She bowed down and waded through the branches, dragging her vehicle deep enough to hide it from sight, then leaned it against a tree. She took off her backpack and helmet and left them under the same tree.

She wanted to make a little foray and explore what was going on at the desolate farm. She had no guarantee that it was the exact location as the place Ben had referred to as The Base, considering that the signal from her phone could be not precise, or he could simply have parked his car away from his destination. However, it looked like a place one could use as a base for some undercover activity. The piles of building materials were a good hiding spot, and people gathering there would look like construction workers.

Amelia put her phone in silent mode and crawled through the trees toward the back side of the farm. Overgrown weeds surrounding the rickety wooden fence allowed her to crawl toward it unnoticed. She peeked through a gap in the fence and saw a wooden barn hiding the farmhouse, so she moved along the fence to her right to have a better point of view. There, she could see a semitruck parked in the yard—an indicator that someone was probably in the house, although she couldn't spot any movement yet. After more thorough observation, Amelia noticed two motorcycles standing near the fence. So more than one person was there.

Things started getting more interesting. Amelia lay on the ground and froze, observing. In ten minutes, two men emerged from the building and lit up cigarettes. They discussed something heatedly, but they were too far to discern any words, nor could she see their faces.

She needed to get closer, and the barn looked like a good hiding spot. The sun had almost set already, so trying to sneak in felt safe. She estimated a gap under the fence was big enough for her to slip through, waited till the smokers went back to the house, and dragged herself through. Her back got scratched, but she made it. On all fours, she rushed toward the barn and took a peek from the corner. The coast was clear. She sat on the ground, leaned against the barn wall, and prepared to wait.

In less than half an hour, she heard the front door open, and somebody strode out with a heavy pace.

"I'm already tired of waiting," someone moaned in a creaky voice. "Why did he gather us here just to sit and wait? He doesn't even know for sure if there will be work for us today or not."

Someone else cut him off. "Shut up, Chicco! All you do is whine like a snotty baby. If you were up for this, you should have realized that it wouldn't be a piece of cake. You're getting paid good money."

The door opened again.

"Hey, bro, what's this fuss about?" asked another person. "You're making my dog nervous." Amelia could hear muffled barking from inside the house.

"Chicco is moping again, and to be honest, I'm already tired of watching his grumpy face. I don't understand why Ben thinks he's a good fit in our team!"

"Hey, guys, why don't we just go inside and watch the match? Time will pass quickly this way."

"Sure. All we do is kill time," Chicco said in his creaky voice.

"Here ya go."

The door opened, and suddenly, the dog's barking got louder.

"Hey, Rokki, what's wrong, boy? Go inside!"

The barking got even louder, and Amelia's heart stopped as she realized she was the reason for the dog's disturbance. Soaked with sweat and adrenaline, she couldn't go undetected by its nose. She was doomed. The thought that they might have a dog had never crossed her mind.

Her muscles made a decision before her brain processed it, and she slid toward the fence and ducked under it headfirst and wiggled like a worm in a desperate attempt to get out, but sudden pain paralyzed her for a moment. Something like hundreds of sharp knives crunched on her ankle.

"Holy crap, guys, Rokki just got an intruder! Good boy, Rokki. You can let go now. I'll deal with him."

Somebody grabbed Amelia's legs and pulled. She tried to resist but to no avail. With her blurred vision, she saw a tall husky man in a black bandana with skulls bent above her as he turned her onto her back. A black bulldog sat at his feet, baring its teeth.

"Huh? A girl!"

Two other men were right there to surround her.

"Who the hell are you, and what are you doing here?" asked Rokki's owner, who seemed to be in charge.

Amelia groaned, clenching the bitten left ankle with ripped jeans fabric around it.

"Hey... I didn't mean any harm, I swear... I just was looking for a place to spend the night, and I thought nobody was living here."

"Then you found a perfect place," snickered a guy in a patched motorcycle vest, exposing his brown teeth. "We'll take you in and give you some love. Won't we, guys?"

"Are you homeless?" asked the bulldog's man. "You don't look like a hobo."

"I'm not homeless. I just got in some trouble… I will explain everything—just let me get on my feet." Amelia made an effort and stood up. Her ankle was hurting, but she was able to stand on it. It wasn't broken or sprained, as she'd feared. She exaggeratedly stumbled and leaned against the fence. "I was traveling to São Paulo, but my car got stolen, and I had no money or phone to make a call… I walked down the street and got lost…" she mumbled, switching her eyes between them.

The third one, probably Chicco, hadn't said a word so far. He stepped back, his arms crossed on his chest, looking bored.

"Poor thing," grinned Black Vest. He creeped closer, devouring her with his eyes.

It didn't look like there was any chance they would just let her go.

Amelia caught a moment when Skull Bandana got distracted by his dog, which howled, unable to sit still. She struck Black Vest between his ribs, in the solar plexus. The blow was precise, and he curled up as she spun on her feet and jumped onto the fence, pulling herself up.

The bulldog dashed after her with a furious snarl, scratching the wood with his claws. She kicked it in the face and jumped over to the other side of the fence. She landed on her feet and rushed toward the grove, away from the light of the lantern at the farm. Adrenaline blocked the pain in her wounded ankle, allowing her to run for her life, out of sight and into the darkness.

The men shouted threats as they jumped over the fence. She didn't turn back, concentrated on speeding up with all the might her muscles could provide. Suddenly, she felt something grab her by a leg, dropping her to the ground—she hadn't noticed a snag in the tall grass. "Stand up and run!" commanded her brain, but her disoriented body could not follow up quickly.

"Gotcha, you bitch!" gloated the black vest, approaching her.

She spun on her back and kicked him in his midsection. He writhed, and the other two, who just turned up, went "Whoa!" in surprise. Amelia pushed herself up with her hands and got back on her feet. She squared up and balanced herself. When Skull Bandana got near enough, she spun on her unharmed foot and kicked him with the other one. It was a clean move, throwing him back, but the next moment, a thrust from behind her pushed her onto the ground.

Black Vest, who landed on her, nailed her down with a knee. He punched her in the face fiercely, almost knocking her out with one blow, followed by another, then one more.

"Taste that, li'l slut!" He stood up and kicked her in the belly.

Her cramping muscles somehow absorbed the blow, but she still felt like she'd been shattered.

"I want to talk to Ben..." she wheezed, blood pouring from her nose. "I have important news for him." She needed to do something to win some time before they beat her to death.

They seemed to be surprised.

"What's your business with Ben?" asked Skull Bandana.

"I can't tell you... It's... it's confidential."

"Ha! You're bluffing!" spat Black Vest. "You were saying something else before!"

"Why did you run?" asked Skull Bandana.

"It's very serious. I couldn't tell you... I was expecting to meet Ben."

"You can talk to us. Ben has no secrets from us."

"Are you sure that you want to know too much? It might be dangerous to your life and health."

They looked at one another, puzzled.

"Okay, get her inside. I'll call Ben and figure things out," commanded Skull Bandana at last.

Black Vest yanked her from the ground and twisted one hand behind her back.

"Move!" he commanded.

They brought her to the house and pushed her onto the ground near the porch. Skull Bandana brought a skein of twine and tied her feet and her wrists behind her back.

While watching her, he drew out a phone and made a call. "Dammit, Ben isn't answering," he spat after several attempts and stared at her with a heavy glare.

"All right, he will get back to us sooner or later. Anyhow, you're not getting anywhere. Chicco, watch her! And you too, Rokki. Sit here!" he commanded and went inside. Black Vest followed him.

The short, sinewy guy that had stayed silent

all that time sat on the step of the porch. He stared at her without any expression on his gaunt face. Amelia stared back, her vision blurred from pain, recovering. Something eye-catching in his face drew her sight, the way that something unusually revolting did. She felt like she'd seen him before, although his face seemed hard to forget, with those peaked cheekbones and peering eyes under heavy eyebrows pierced with two steel rings.

"You're Amelia, right?" he said in his creaky voice. "Amelia del Atore," he continued after getting no response. He chuckled. "That's funny, such a valuable trophy coming to us by itself."

Amelia preferred to keep silent, wondering whether revealing herself or denying it would be better. Before she could come to a decision, he got up and headed to the gate, treading softly, and opened it without making any sound. She heard the roar of a motorcycle engine as he took off.

His two sidekicks burst out onto the porch, alarmed by the noise and the dog barking.

"Shut up, Rokki! What the hell... Where is Chicco?" yelled Skull Bandana. He glanced at Amelia, who lay still and silent. "Damn, this bastard is dead!"

He made another futile attempt at a phone call, swore loudly, and lit a cigarette.

"Told ya he was trouble!" said Black Vest, taking out his own pack of cigarettes.

"Oh, shut up," scoffed his sidekick and took a long drag. "This all stinks bad. Who knows what this little rat is up to? If Ben doesn't answer in half an hour, we'll wrap up and be gone."

"What about her?" Black Vest nodded at Amelia.

"We will see."

She couldn't tell how long they sat on the porch, smoking cigarette after cigarette. At some moments, her consciousness blacked out, but then a sharp pain brought her back to reality.

When she heard a voice magnified by a loudspeaker exclaim, "You are surrounded by the police. Put your hands above your heads and move to the exit!" she wasn't sure whether it was real or just a hallucination her exhausted mind had created.

Her two captors cursed.

"You are at gunpoint. Don't make any sudden moves, or we will shoot with no second warning!"

Amelia rolled behind the porch and curled up. As through a fog, she heard the sound of hustle and fuss and a gunshot at the distance, followed by a high-pitched dog squeal. Then Marcelu's voice exclaimed her name. She turned her head and saw his frowning, dismayed face as he kneeled near her.

"You're... you're all covered in blood..." he muttered.

"Step away, son. You're not helping," Captain Diego Campras uttered in an annoyed voice. He took an army knife out of his pocket and carefully cut the ropes binding Amelia's wrists and ankles.

She rose to her knees, staggering. Her hands were numb, and she couldn't move her fingers.

"Call Mom. We're taking her to the hospital,"

commanded Diego. He grabbed Amelia, pulled her onto his shoulder, stood up and moved toward the gate.

Marcelu helped him to place her in the backseat of a police car then sat next to her, holding her head on his knees.

"Everything is fine. You'll be all right," he said, lightly stroking her hair with his fingertips. "I tracked your signal to that farm, and then it was lost. I got so scared."

"My phone... I guess I dropped it in a fight, and it switched off. I'm sorry."

"It's all right now. You are safe. We are going to the hospital. My mom will meet us there and take care of you."

"Uh-huh," grunted Amelia.

"She is an experienced surgeon. You will be in good hands. Whatever you have broken, she will fix it."

Amelia closed her eyes and heard Marcelu's disturbed voice screaming in her ear: "Hey, don't pass out! Look at me! I need to know that you are all right! Amelia!"

She made an effort and raised her eyelids.

"That's better. My mom will check you, and after that, you can have a rest. I know it's been tough. Please, hold on just a little bit more."

They drove to the hospital parking lot where Amelia had been just a few hours before. Diego carried her to the entrance and placed her on a gurney. A tall woman with chestnut hair wrapped in a bun and wearing light-blue scrubs approached them at a quick pace.

"Hi, Amelia. My name is Isaura. Can you tell me what happened to you?" she asked sympathetically, bending over her.

"Dog bit me on my leg, and then... its owners kicked and punched me." She placed her hand on her stomach. "It feels like everything is smashed inside."

Isaura frowned. "We'll get a quick X-ray now and then put stitches on your ankle. When was your last tetanus vaccination?"

"It seems I got all of them on time..."

"Was it the bulldog that officer Andrade shot that bit you?" asked Marcelu.

She nodded.

"I guess we should have it tested for rabies."

"I'll make a request to a forensic team," said Diego.

Isaura nodded to him. "You can go now. I'll drive the kids home when we're finished."

"Okay. I need to get back to my guys. Call me when you have any news." He headed toward the exit at a fast pace then turned. "Don't submit any paperwork on her for now."

"Got it." His wife nodded.

After forty minutes and countless injections, Isaura informed her, "You have a crack in one of your ribs and a huge hematoma on your abdomen, but overall, it's not so bad. Your nose is not broken, but it may be swollen for several days. Could be much worse."

"Yay. How lucky I am," Amelia said drowsily, lying on a couch in hospital pajamas that had replaced her clothes, dirty with dust and blood. Her left ankle stitched and bandaged, she was feeling light-headed from anesthesia or blood loss or probably both.

The smell of the medical office saturated with disinfectants, spirit, and medicines seemed calming and pleasant. Her consciousness was switching off time and again, but it felt like the world was friendly and safe again. Marcelu placed her in a wheelchair and took her to Isaura's car.

Finally, she found herself in a soft bed under a blanket, where she was allowed to let her exhausted mind switch off. But in her sleep, she continued to run and fight and fall and run again and again.

CHAPTER FIFTEEN

WHEN AMELIA OPENED HER EYES, she needed a while to figure out where she was. Bright sunlight slipping through the dense curtain let her see the room contained a desk; bookshelves with textbooks, awards, and a globe; posters of heavy metal bands; a periodic table; and a map of Brazil.

Amelia made an attempt to sit up in bed, and her body reacted with a jolt of pain. She moaned, pushing herself up with her hands, and finally got her feet to the floor. The door, which was ajar, opened, and Marcelu entered.

"Oh, you woke up! How are you feeling?"

"As if I was trampled by a horse," she responded grumpily.

He frowned sympathetically. "No wonder. You

will need some time to recover.”

“Is this your room?” asked Amelia.

Marcelu nodded.

She looked at the sleeping bag with pillow and blanket, lying on the floor. “Did you sleep here on the floor?”

“Yes, just in case you needed some help at night. You screamed in your sleep.”

“Oh. Sorry I caused you and your family so much trouble.” She sighed.

“Don’t say that. It’s not your fault. And I’m always happy to take care of you.” Marcelu cautiously sat on the bed next to her.

Amelia looked at her lap. “I was an idiot. You were right. I shouldn’t have gone there.”

“Well, if it makes you feel better, the police found tons of evidence against these guys. They had whole boxes of guns and ammunition and, supposedly, drugs.”

“Oh, that’s interesting!” She raised her head, invigorated.

“Yeah, my dad is still on duty. They’re searching the farm and interrogating those two brats.”

Amelia looked at a digital clock on the desk. It showed 10:15 a.m.

“Mom went to work at the hospital, so it’s only you and me now,” said Marcelu. He glanced at her and quickly looked away. “She told me to make chicken soup for you. Do you want some? It’s very good for recuperating.”

“Thanks. Maybe later. So, what about those two? Did they admit anything?”

"I don't know any details yet, but it seems like you stirred up a hornet's nest. They definitely were planning something huge. Too bad their gang leader didn't get caught. But I have tracked him up to Roseira. He was there this morning, and then the signal was gone."

Amelia winced. "Battery must have died. It lasted long enough, not like these modern smartphones. I guess he will figure out that his gang members got arrested and will lie low."

"However, I have a track of his itinerary for more than twenty-four hours. That's already something. I will hand that over to my dad when I have a chance. That was a smooth trick with that phone."

"At least I was of some use other than being a troublemaker." Amelia heard a plaintive whining and scratching behind the door. "What is that? You have a dog?"

"Yeah, I guess she wants to go outside. By the way, my mom got in touch with your parents today."

Amelia frowned. "And?"

"They know that you've been through some scrape but are now safe and sound. They are in São Paulo now but are going to be here by the end of the day."

"Okay. I guess I'm gonna get some more punches from my mom," concluded Amelia grumpily.

Marcelu suppressed a chuckle. "I believe you. Your mom can be... um, stringent sometimes. I don't know— try to pretend that you have amnesia after hitting your head and don't recognize her."

Amelia made an odd sound. "I don't believe that

will work as an excuse with her. And don't make me laugh. My ribs hurt badly."

Marcelu headed to the door. "Come on, Princess, stop whining."

"What? I'm not whining!" Amelia protested, outraged.

Marcelu turned and looked at her in confusion. "I was talking to the dog. Her name is Princess Celestia."

"Oh..."

"But if you want, I can call you Princess as well."

"There's no need for that, thank you. But please let her go outside. I hate dogs. I had a rather unpleasant encounter with one of them lately."

Marcelu raised his eyebrows. "Ugh... but you can't hate our Princess. She's the sweetest pup in the world." He opened the door, and a big fluffy Airedale terrier jumped into his embrace. "Let's go, Princy."

Amelia leaned on the bed and pushed herself to her feet and took some tentative steps toward the door. Her left ankle was swollen, but she was able to make her way out of the bedroom, limping slightly.

Marcelu saw her as he returned from the yard and moved toward her. "Do you need a hand?" he asked, seemed concerned.

"No, I'm fine. Where is the bathroom?"

"Here." He opened the door and turned on the light for her.

Amelia's eyes met with her reflection in the mirror, which startled her. She needed a moment to realize that the swollen face, with dark-purple bruises covering most of its left half and the split lip covered with dried blood, was her own. No wonder Marcelu averted his eyes each time he looked at her.

She carefully washed her face with cold water, combed her hair back with her fingers, and looked in the mirror again. It was still her face, and her bruises were proof that she'd survived a battle. She'd been tried by fire, and no one could intimidate her now. Her reflection looked at her with approval.

"So, what about soup?" called Marcelu, appearing in the kitchen doorway.

"Sounds good," agreed Amelia. She proceeded to the kitchen and sat on one of the chairs near the round table. "You have such nice plants," she said, admiring the pots with proliferating vegetation at three windows.

"Yeah, my mom likes them." Marcelu placed a bowl with soup in front of her. "Hope you like it. I cooked it myself."

"Very good," said Amelia after taking a spoonful. "I haven't eaten since yesterday's afternoon, before I left Itajubá... Oh, I left a motorcycle I borrowed and other stuff in a grove near that farm," she realized. "I need to get it back and return to the owner before somebody steals it."

"Stay home today. I'll deal with it."

"You don't know where it is, exactly."

"There are police and forensics searching the place. Dad called the feds for backup, as it looks pretty serious, and your father would insist on it anyway."

"Oh!" Amelia put the spoon back in the bowl and frowned as she remembered something important. "That guy, Chicco... He recognised me and said that they were hunting me or something like this. I'm sure it was them who attacked me that night!"

Marcelu looked at her in consternation. "You said Chicco?"

"Yes, he's the only one whose name I heard. Creepy fella."

"What did he look like?"

"Rather short, swarthy... Such an unpleasant bony face, horselike I would say if you can forgive the rude simile. Has a piercing in his right eyebrow."

Marcelu took a phone from his pocket, sat on a chair next to her, and did a quick search.

"Is this him?" He showed her a picture on the screen.

"Yes! Do you know him?" Amelia raised her eyebrows.

"I do... better than I would like to." Marcelu pressed his joined hands against his chin and took a deep breath. "I guess I have to tell you something."

"What?" Amelia frowned and stared at him.

"A few days before the graduation party, I took my dad's car to have the air filter replaced at the service. He never had time to do it himself. Chicco is my old friend, and he works at the service, so I went to him, and I discussed with him that I was going to invite you for a trip after the party..."

"Really? You discuss with your mates how to better hook up with gals?"

Marcelu shrugged. "Well, you know, sometimes we

all need someone to talk to. The point is that I mentioned your name to him, and he knew it was very likely that you would be with me that night... And then it happened... and it looked like they knew you would walk down that street and waited there for you."

Amelia's eyes widened in realization. "So you knew, and you didn't say anything about Chicco?"

"I wanted to talk with him myself first. It could've been just a coincidence. And if he got called to the police for interrogation... Well, you met him, and you know what he is like. He has a talent of making everybody hate him."

"Not much of a talent!"

"Yes, but he's exceptional at it. He alienates people around him wherever he goes. He dropped out of school when he was fourteen. He got severely bullied. His own mother abandoned him, leaving him with his grandma, and then his grandma kicked him out of her home. He got beaten and kicked out at several places he worked at, for no specific reason. Many people just can't stand him—I don't know why exactly—maybe because of his annoying demeanor or the unpleasant face you noted or both. Besides that, he's gay, and it's known in the town, so I didn't want him to have any unnecessary encounters with police, for it could end up really bad for him."

Amelia looked at him doubtfully. "So, did you talk to him?"

"I couldn't reach him. He didn't answer the phone. I went to the auto service he worked at, but they said he quit, which wasn't something out of the ordinary, considering he didn't last long in any of his jobs, so I decided to wait for a while. Maybe it wasn't the best decision, but he's my friend, and I know that behind his defiance and unpleasant exterior, he's a decent guy, and I can rely on him. Or at least I used to believe that."

"Well, now you know why you couldn't find him—he was too busy with his gang buddies," scoffed Amelia.

Marcelu put his hands on his head. "I still can't believe he could do that... Why? Did he do anything to you?"

"Actually... no. He was there, but he remained passive all the time, just stood behind those other guys. And then... they went inside and told him to guard me. And that's when he told me he recognized me and left right after, which his sidekicks were very pissed off about. I realize now that was weird but can't really explain his behavior. It looked like he didn't want to stain his hands with my blood, but he didn't try to help me either. He could've released me and taken me with him on his motorcycle if he wanted, but he just fled."

"That's why he wasn't there when the police arrived." Marcelu frowned. "Slick bastard. Not going to cover his ass anymore. I will tell my dad everything, I think."

"Finally!" Amelia raised a thumb.

"I feel terrible now." Marcelu glanced at her and lowered his head. "It's like I undermined your safety for his sake."

"Don't think like that! The only one you sabotaged is yourself. Had you said anything about that conversation with Chicco, you would avoid getting suspected, but it wouldn't have changed anything for me. Even if the police had started looking for Chicco, there's no guarantee they would've succeeded. I don't regret that everything turned out this way. Now we have those two arrested, and I hope they will testify and reveal all the members of their clique."

Marcelu looked at her with pity. "Even if they would, it doesn't justify the price."

"Come on. Don't be dramatic! I'm trying to be optimistic here. Can't I praise myself for the positive outcome of the skirmish I got into? Maybe the police will give me a reward, something like a certificate for being the best bait of the year." She tried to smile, but her lips were cracked, and the smile turned out wry.

Marcelu grimaced. "Sorry, but I can't see anything funny about this. Nothing would ever be worth exposing your life to so much danger."

"It seems like you got hurt more than I got battered. See, I'm alive and going to be fine soon. Don't look at me like I'm dying."

"Sorry, I just can't..." Marcelu stood up and looked out the window. "I can't see you in this state. It makes my heart bleed." He made an effort and turned toward her. "Why should it have been you? You are so delicate and so fine, with skin like rose petals. I can't see it covered with bruises."

Amelia gasped and looked at him in a daze. "You talk about me like I'm a thing," she said finally. "Like I'm your new car you don't want to see scratched. I'm not some decorative thing for amusing people's eyes. Even if

I'm not as pretty as you liked to see me, this abominable me is still me."

"What are you talking about? Goodness gracious!" yelled Marcelu, "It just hurts me to see you hurt, and I want to kill those scumbags when I think of what they did to you."

Amelia rose to her feet, placed her hands on Marcelu's shoulders, and looked into his eyes.

"Marcelu, dear. I'm here with you, and I'm fine. You saved me, and nothing really bad happened. All these bruises will heal very soon. Your care makes me feel safe and sheltered, but don't pity me, please."

Marcelu put his hands on her back and gently pulled her close. She felt his warmth, and a wave of tenderness washed away the tension between them.

"I didn't mean to say that you were abominable," Marcelu muttered in her ear. "It's not your face that makes you beautiful. It is the fire in your eyes, and it's still on."

She leaned back and smiled at him. "And I feel even more fierce and brazen now, when I know what I'm worth."

Marcelu beamed. "That's my girl!"

CHAPTER SIXTEEN

"HOW ARE YOU TWO DOING HERE?" asked Diego, entering the living room.

"Pretty good. Just watching a movie!" Marcelu muted the TV, which was playing a foreign show, and stood up from the sofa. "I cooked *coxinhas* for dinner. They are warm in the oven. You must be hungry."

"He is so handy." Amelia smiled as she lay on a sofa, covered with a throw. "It was a delight to see him mixing the dough and cooking—such neat work."

Marcelu gave her a cross glance.

"That's all I did, just lay here and watched him. I wouldn't be much use anyway. I can't even grill a sausage without burning it."

"Good to see you're feeling better, Amelia," said Diego, carefully looking at her. "Also, we've found your motorcycle and bag. Here." He took the backpack off his shoulder and put it on the floor. "The motorcycle is in my truck. I brought it."

"Oh, thank you so much!" she said with relief.

"Your mom just called me. They are approaching Lindageral and will be here in half an hour."

"Oh my!" Amelia closed her eyes.

Diego snickered and headed to his room. He changed from his uniform to casual clothes and finished a plate of coxinhas and a bowl of soup by the time a knock on the door announced the arrival of the guests. The captain stood to welcome them. Amelia pulled herself to a half-sitting position and got wrapped in the throw. She put on sunglasses that clearly did not cover even half of the damage done to her face but served as a shield for her confidence.

Robert and Lucrecia entered the room, followed by Diego.

"Oh dear..." remarked Lucrecia.

"Amelia, dear, how are you feeling?" asked Robert, approaching her. He bowed down and kissed her on the top of her head.

"I'm fine, Dad. Got in some fuss but got off with some minor bruises. Sorry for making you worry."

"That's fine, sweetheart. We understand your struggles."

"No, we don't," objected Lucrecia, crossing her arms over her chest. "Some explanations might be in order."

"For sure, carinho, but I believe we have more

urgent things to talk about," said Robert mildly.

Diego backed him. "Right. I believe all of us have important news to share, so let's have a kind of conference to get updated and brainstorm what we know. Have a seat, please." He waved toward the corner sofa.

Amelia's parents complied and took spots near their daughter. The captain took a notepad and pen from the counter and put them on a coffee table.

"You too, Marcelu. Have a seat," he commanded his son, who was humbly standing aside and observing. "As these two young people actively participated in the latest events and have proven themselves to be reasonable, I believe we should include them in the discussion."

Robert nodded energetically. Lucrecia scoffed and rolled her eyes but did not say anything.

"All right then." The captain cleared his throat and opened his notebook. "Amelia did a great job tracking down a nest of the criminal gang at the abandoned farm on Cordeira Road. Two guys we arrested, Reinaldo Alvarez and Erik Pinho, had been convicted of severe crimes before: armed robberies, grievous bodily harm, torture, homicide in the case of Pinho. We found a full range of weaponry, from knives to rifles with two boxes of ammo."

"Holy smokes!" blurted Robert.

"Yeah, those guys were clearly up to nothing good. But it's also clear that they were just mercenaries. One of them refused to talk, but the other one, Alvarez, cracked and told us that last night, they were preparing a raid in Gerdau. They got an order to attack the home of the owner of the local branch of Burger Queen restaurants. Of course, he swore that that was their first assignment, which they failed to accomplish, and blamed everything on their flagman, Ben. But quick research revealed that there were previous attacks on owners of this franchise in other cities, so we can track this sequence."

"I was tracking Ben by the phone Amelia left in his car," explained Marcelu. "I lost him when the battery died, but the last location I spotted was near Roseira, which is on the road to Gerdau."

"Is it worth asking how you came to leave your phone in his car, Amelia?" asked Lucrecia, eloquently raising an eyebrow.

"Well, long story short, I started working in a restaurant in Itajubá, and I noticed a group of guys that seemed to be harassing its owner. I overheard one of them mentioning 'a base in Lindagerale' while talking on the phone, so I distracted him in a conversation and dropped my phone in his car."

"Restaurant in Itajubá?" Lucrecia snickered. "I remember you threatened to go as far as Roraima Mountain."

"It was in my further plans," retorted Amelia.

"Oh, you found a job. Good for you!" Robert told her. "See, I told you she would be fine," he said, turning to his wife.

"So I tracked his location in Lindageral and went for a quick exploration," continued Amelia. She decided not to bring Lucrecia's wrath down on Marcelu's head by mentioning his involvement.

Lucrecia gave a weary sigh. "Did I hear this right, that you found out there are some really bad people planning some very bad things and decided to see it in person? Makes total sense!"

"Mom! Can we please talk over the facts first?" protested Amelia. "You will have plenty of time to reprimand me later."

Diego got to his feet and retrieved a bottle of wine with three glasses from the kitchen cupboard. "For better concentration." He winked as he put the glasses on the coffee table and poured wine in them.

"Just an ounce for me. I'm driving," Robert warned him.

Lucrecia took a big gulp from her glass.

"So... back to the events of last night," continued Diego, "Amelia was very smart to have Marcelu track her phone, and he was able to react promptly. He contacted me to inform me that Amelia was in danger. Also, there was an anonymous call to 190 at ten thirty-five p.m. I assume that was you as well?" he asked, turning to his son.

Marcelu looked at him in surprise. "No. I just called you. It didn't occur to me to call in an emergency."

"Who could it be, then?" Diego raised an eyebrow. "Maybe neighbors who heard screams?"

Amelia and Marcelu exchanged questioning looks.

"Anything is possible." Marcelu shrugged.

"Anyway, it's good that we got there on time," the captain resumed. "Now, we have those two in our custody, and they can help us unravel the whole network.

Oh, and I almost forgot a bit of important news—Pinho's fingerprints matched the ones found on the body of the late Marinio Risso, on his watch and belt buckle."

"Aha!" exclaimed Marcelu.

"We'll perform more in-depth research, including analysis of his knife, to detect blood particles, but we already have enough on him to charge him with this murder, as well as the murder of that guy who was found stubbed near your estate. The pattern was pretty much similar. He was identified as Tadeu Peres and also had a rich criminal background."

"Oh, thank goodness!" said Lucrecia. "Who in the name of sanity could imagine Amelia doing this?"

"Yes, and Luis Sanches, who was our primary suspect in Risso's murder, is also getting released as soon as we get the paperwork done."

"Oh, Elvina's boyfriend." Amelia winced. "I hope he won't start bugging her now."

"We'll take care of her," Marcelu assured her as his father nodded in affirmation.

"Such a relief to know these murders are solved! Cheers to that!" Lucrecia raised her glass, and the two men followed her lead.

"We also have some important news," declared Lucrecia after emptying her glass. "A great deal of it, actually."

"Did you bring that car tycoon to light?" asked Diego.

Robert shook his head slowly. "It turned out to be more complex than that. I had an intense face-to-face conversation with both Lando Lacerdo and Bruno Carvalho. I told Lando that I suspect Bruno, and vice versa, so if one of them was planning to frame the other, I would make him believe he'd reached his goal."

"That's how you play this," Diego said approvingly. "What were the results?"

"Bruno was absolutely outraged. He suggested excluding Lando from the deal and placing the order for the manufacture of the mechanical part of the robo-harvester with a foreign company. Whereas Lando told me that he'd detected some spy activity in his corporate network."

"Eh?"

"It looked like somebody had hacked in and tried to intercept data specifically related to the harvester, and he suspected someone from his company had done it. So we planned a giveaway. Lando and I met with his managers one-on-one and leaked some information that would trigger certain actions on Bruno's side. It was something I wouldn't normally do." He exchanged glances with his wife. "But in this case, we had to play rough."

Captain moved in his seat impatiently. "Okay, okay, so what's the result?"

"There was no result. The leak didn't seem to go through, so either none of the people in question was connected with Bruno, or they outsmarted us."

"Hmm..."

Robert continued, "And then we found something that made us look at this at a completely different light."

Lucrecia nodded. "I performed a thorough

cleaning of Robert's office in our São Paulo home, and I found a spy listening device on the top of a cabinet."

"What?" yelled Amelia, staring at her with her mouth agape.

"Yes, right in our home! We invited a private expert—decided not to involve the police for now—but he couldn't detect where it was transmitting its signal. All he could do was make sure we didn't have more bugs."

Amelia looked at her parents in disbelief. "But who could do that?"

"Good question." Lucrecia nodded. "Our first thought, obviously, was that either Bruno or Lando did this while they were in Robert's office. But on second thought, that didn't sound realistic. None of them was left in the office alone or could do it unnoticed in the presence of two people, including Robert himself. During the party, none of the guests went upstairs. I think I would've noticed."

"The only obvious suspect was Theresa, our housekeeper. She came to clean the house once a week, sometimes in our absence. Robert kept his office locked, but the lock is quite primitive, and I'm sure it could be undone, given some time with no supervision."

"For how long did she work for you?" asked Diego, frowning.

"That's the thing—she just started a few months ago! The lady that helped us before moved to the north to look after her sick mother and recommended Theresa to me. She provided me with references, but I was too sloppy to check them properly. Now she's disappeared, and her phone is blocked."

"Yes, it seems like she was an infiltrator." The captain nodded.

"But that very likely means that Bruno Carvalho and Lando Lacerdo could be both innocent of the burglary and the following events and there was a completely different power in action," noted Robert.

They all looked at one another in silence for a moment.

"Well, that's a bit of relief, isn't it?" muttered Diego.

Robert hesitated. "It is, for sure, but there's still this very hostile other power."

"Well, I guess you knew that you would be at gunpoint when you took over the company, let alone when you went into politics."

"And we will take the challenge," stated Lucrecia before Robert could say anything. "You should have seen me this week when I scanned every corner of our home with a special anti-spy detector. Thank goodness, there wasn't anything in our Lindageral estate. But we also have the most advanced security system in both our homes. I guess that's the reason why Theresa couldn't remove the bug—I warned her that I would need to meet her in order to give her access, and soon after that, she disappeared."

"You need to be very careful now," resumed Diego. "And speaking of that, we decided to keep Amelia out of sight as much as possible. We took her to the hospital yesterday, and Isaura provided her all the necessary help. It wasn't her shift, but there were no other patients then, so she could arrange everything without drawing attention, and she hasn't made any official records."

Both Robert and Lucrecia nodded eagerly.

"I can't express how grateful we are to you and Isaura for taking care of our daughter," said Lucrecia, putting a hand to her heart.

"Yes, thank you so much," Amelia echoed her, embarrassed and sneaking a glance at Marcelu, who was silently observing and nodded with a slight smile.

"We discussed it between us and decided that it's better if Amelia stays with us for a little while, until things get clearer," said Diego. "It would hardly occur to anyone to look for her here. And Isaura can change the dressings on her leg."

Amelia answered her parents' worried look with "I got slightly chewed by a bulldog."

Robert looked at the captain. "Are you sure it will be convenient for you?"

He nodded. "Marcelu doesn't have much to do till February, when his university course starts, so he can look after Amelia. And these two seem to make a very efficient team, investigating the gang activity, so let them brainstorm together. Who knows? Maybe they will solve the case..." Diego's moustaches moved in a grin.

Amelia and Marcelu exchanged surprised glances.

Diego raised a finger. "As long as you don't take over the business of the police and don't break the law."

The two newly proclaimed investigators nodded hesitantly.

***

"I was surprised my mom allowed me to stay here without any objections," noted Amelia when her parents were gone.

Marcelu shrugged. "Well, I guess she realized already that she can't just tell you what to do."

"Right. It only took me spending about two weeks away from home and getting into a fight with gangsters." Amelia smirked. "By the way, I need to return the motorcycle I took to the owner." She reached into her backpack, searched its pockets, and finally took out a notebook. "May I use your phone? I need to make a call."

Marcelu nodded and handed her a cell phone.

After a few futile attempts, Amelia put the phone aside and frowned. "Darn. She isn't answering."

Marcelu raised his eyebrows in a silent question.

"Fortunata, the girl I stayed with in Itajubá. She is... going through some complicated stuff in her life as well, and I'm worried if she's okay."

"Oh... I hope she'll call back. By the way, that reminded me of Elvina..."

"Right, her pushy boyfriend goes free now. What are we going to do about that?"

"Obviously, talk to her first and ask what she thinks about it." Marcelu raised his phone and typed a couple of messages then sat next to Amelia and showed her the screen.

"'I know it was you who called the police to rescue Amelia. Please, get in touch. I want to help you,'" she read and raised her eyes to Marcelu. "To Chicco?"

He nodded.

"Yes, I thought of this too. It seems very unlikely that neighbors could hear something—there are hardly any neighbors."

"Hope he will respond."

Marcelu's phone vibrated, and he unlocked the screen.

"Is it him?" asked Amelia in excitement.

"Nope. It's Elvina. She's home now and says I can come over. Is it okay if I leave? Mom will be here any minute."

"What? There's no way you're going without me!" screamed Amelia, pushing the throw off her lap.

Marcelu frowned. "It's been discussed that it's better for you to stay put for now."

"You're driving there, I assume. I'll quickly sneak in and out of the car so nobody can see me. Really, Marcelu, I can't just sit and do nothing while nothing is solved yet."

He sighed. "Goodness gracious, you just can't live without trouble, can you?"

Amelia shrugged with an innocuous smile on her face.

"All right, let's go, but quickly, before my parents see us."

"Sure!" Amelia took a hoodie from her backpack and pulled it on, covering her head.

"Okay."

Marcelu nodded in affirmation of her look—

sunglasses and the hood hiding most of her face. He took keys from the dresser near the entrance, and they went outside to the blue Honda Civic parked near the gate.

CHAPTER SEVENTEEN

"THANKS FOR COMING!" ELVINA SMILED, opening the door for them. Then she noted Amelia and was stunned for a moment.

"Hey, Elvina. It's me, Amelia," she said, taking off the hood. "Sorry. Didn't want to startle you. Never mind my crazy look. I had an accident, but I'm fine now."

"Oh... All right. I just didn't expect to see you. Come in, please!" she gestured to them.

They followed her to the kitchen.

"You already met Camilla, our accountant, right?"

A blond girl wearing in a short-sleeved gray dress with a white collar lifted her eyes from some papers on the table and waved at them with a smile. "Nice to meet you guys again."

"Camilla helped me so much I just can't thank

her enough!" said Elvina, pulling out two more chairs for them. "If you or someone you know ever needs an accountant, she's the best you can think of!"

Camilla smiled. "Thanks, Elvina. Don't think I have capacity for new clients, though. I'm already doing accounting for eighty-three companies."

"How's everything going?" asked Marcelu as they sat at the table.

"I don't want to jinx it, but it looks like I'm coping. I've gotten so much help from everyone around me that I just can't fail you all."

"But it's mostly your achievement, dear," Camilla reassured her.

"I was so afraid I couldn't manage! I could never imagine running a business myself," confessed Elvina. "I started driving a car and even a cargo van! I got a license last year but was too scared to drive. It turns out I can do it!"

"Wow, that's amazing!" Amelia said. "I can imagine how it feels."

"It feels fantastic. I can't believe I'm doing it!"

"Glad everything's going well," Marcelu summed up. "I just wanted to give you a heads-up that Luis will probably be released any day now."

The smile faded from Elvina's face.

"Maybe you heard what happened yesterday night?"

Elvina nodded. "I heard some of the customers talking about the police raid on some abandoned farm, like they caught drug dealers there or something, if that's what you mean."

"Yes. And there is solid evidence that one of the blokes they arrested is the one who killed your father." Marcelu stopped to let that news sink in. "It's kind of insider information, but I thought you needed to hear it as soon as possible."

"Yes... Thank you," said Elvina, turning pale.

"And we want you to know that if Luis starts to bother you, we'll be always by your side to kick his ass," concluded Amelia.

"For sure. Just let us know!" said Marcelu.

"Thank you... It's just so unexpected." Elvina covered her mouth with her hands, letting out a convulsive sob.

Camilla put a hand on her shoulder with a sorrowful look on her face. "That's all right. That's all right... They got those bastards. Now our town will be safe again." She looked at Amelia's bruised face. "I heard you had some kind of accident? I'm really sorry to hear."

"Yes." Amelia touched her cheekbone. "But it's not worth worrying about. I'm really fine."

"It's just so unthinkable that such things happen in our small town," said Camilla. "I moved here from São Paulo two years ago with my sick mother in the hope that the peace of a small quiet town would be better for us both. And now all this is happening!"

"I have lived in Lindageral for all my life, and usually it is quiet and safe," Marcelu assured her. "And hopefully, it will be back to normal soon."

"Let's hope." Camilla nodded sadly.

Elvina stood up, took two mugs from the cupboard, filled them with coffee from a pot, and placed them in front of her guests. "I never believed Luis did it," she said, sitting back in her chair next to Camilla. "I mean, he's a jerk, and now I realize I don't want him anymore. But he's not someone who would stab a living person ten times."

"Well, I guess you know him better than any of us," admitted Marcelu.

"Actually, now I remember some things that occurred before my father died." Elvina mechanically rolled a sugar dispenser in her hands, looking in front of her. "I didn't mention them when the police questioned me. It just went out of my mind completely. I didn't think it was important. But now, all this going on makes me think about it again."

"Would you like to share it with us?" asked Marcelu.

"Yes." The girl nodded. "Honestly, I absolutely don't want to go to the police and talk to them again unless I have to. I was talking about it with Camilla when you came. I need somebody smart to tell me if it's worth bringing up or not."

"You can talk to us. We won't tell anybody without your permission," Marcelu assured her.

Amelia nodded in agreement.

"Well... It looked like my father got a new buddy just about a month before he got killed. Or maybe more—I don't quite remember. But I saw him several times talking with some strange guy after the store closure, and I saw Father leaving with him somewhere in his car a couple times. I've never seen him before. He's not local, I'm sure—when you work with people, you remember faces.

"When I asked Father, he just shushed me, told me they had some business together, but it wasn't my concern. When he talked in that tone, I always knew it was better not to talk back, so I didn't."

"Have you heard what they talked about?" asked Marcelu.

"No. But I noticed that guy left a pack of flyers promoting one of the candidates for the deputy elections, so maybe he wanted us to hand them out or something."

"What's his name?" frowned Amelia. "I mean, of the guy with the flyers."

"I don't know any of them, so I didn't remember."

"My father is one of the candidates, but I don't remember the names of his opponents," admitted Amelia. "But of course he's hoping he can count on the voices of Lindageral's people who know him well, at least. I'm curious who this boor is, who's trying to steal them."

Elvina stood up from her chair. "I think I put them somewhere with old newspapers. I'll try to find them." She went out and returned with a flyer in a minute.

"Aha! Leonardo Solas!" Amelia read the name by the portrait of a young man in a modern navy-blue fitted suit, with a wide, alluring smile on his face.

"Well, I believe it's not against the law to spread campaign materials," Marcelu pointed out gingerly.

"I know. Just... That guy freaked the hell out of me," said Elvina. "The way he looked at me... I got so scared that I was afraid to approach him the next time.

He was bald and had a spooky tattoo of a spider on his nape..."

"A spider!" Amelia squinted.

"What about it?" asked Marcelu.

"I just remembered I saw a very unpleasant man with a tattoo like this recently. Was it a spider with a skull instead of its head?"

"A skull!" blurted Elvina. "Yes, that's why it scared me so much. I hate skulls, skeletons, and such stuff."

"And he was about my height, muscular, with slightly red skin and wrinkles on his neck?"

Elvina nodded "Yes, as far as I remember."

"Where did you see him?" Marcelu asked, turning to Amelia.

"In the restaurant in Itajubá where I worked. He came to talk to the owner."

Marcelu raised his eyebrow. "Oh! That's definitely interesting. Elvina, can you remember anything else about that man? Like when did you see him for the first time? Or what car was he driving?"

"I'm trying to remember..."

A knock on the door interrupted her thought process, and she went to answer.

"Senhora Dolores!" she called out as she opened the door.

"Good evening, sweetheart. Is Camilla with you?" asked a woman.

"Yes, come in, please!"

Elvina returned, followed by a morbidly thin hunched woman with a disoriented look on her pale face.

The skin on her cheeks and ears was blemished with scars, as though she'd had some vile disease.

"Thank God, Milly. I was so worried. It's getting late already."

"Mom!" Camilla stood from her chair and raised her hands imploringly. "It's only eight p.m., for God's sake! I'm not a little girl. I'm twenty-four years old."

"Sorry, sweetheart. It's such a troubled time now. I just couldn't help worrying. I tried to call, but you didn't answer."

"My phone was in my bag. I didn't hear it. Sorry. Did you walk all the way from home?"

The woman nodded.

"You could at least call a taxi!" Camilla turned to the table. "I'm sorry, Elvina. It looks like we're finished for now anyway. I'll drive my mom home."

Elvina nodded. "It's okay. No worries at all. I understand."

Camilla placed her bag on her shoulder and took Dolores by the arm, and they walked out.

"Poor Senhora Dolores," sighed Elvina.

"What's that?" asked Amelia, unplunging from her thoughts. The older woman looked strangely familiar to her, though it took her a while to remember the strange lady who'd approached her near the school before the graduation party. The memory felt like it had happened ages before, and she could hardly see her face back then.

Elvina winced. "She's slightly... unhinged. But she's a good person, always so kind to everyone, and she loves her daughter so much. Camilla is her only one, so it's hard for her to look after her sometimes."

"Oh, I see..." Amelia nodded sympathetically. "I met her before in town. She was saying strange things."

"Ah, that happens to her." Elvina shrugged. "We should be more forgiving to people like her. We never know what disaster may strike ourselves."

***

"Do you believe that somebody can predict the future?" Amelia asked Marcelu on their way home.

"Really?" he scoffed, glancing at her in disbelief. "Of course not."

"Me neither. But here's the thing, I remembered that when I met Senhora Dolores, she told me to beware just before I was attacked on the graduation-party night."

"Beware of what?"

"Of something evil."

"Not very specific," Marcelu said skeptically.

"Maybe mentally impaired people can see such things?"

"The thing is, if somebody predicts something bad to happen, sooner or later their predicament inevitably comes true, and in retrospective it looks like they could see it. That's how it works with all these seers like Nostradamus and Wolf Messing. People remember those who happened to be right several times—which is statistically not so unlikely if you keep forecasting disasters—and forget those who weren't."

"Yep. I guess you're right." Amelia bit her lip.

"It seems like I started losing my marbles with all this happening."

"Don't worry about this." Marcelu smiled. "I'm here to help you pick up your marbles."

When they entered the house, Isaura met them with a furious look.

"What do you think you're doing, son? It's been decided that Amelia stays home for at least a few days."

"Sorry, Isaura. It's not his fault." Amelia raised her palms in a resigning gesture. "I asked him to take me for a ride. I was feeling sick from being locked inside."

"It's been less than twenty-four hours that you've been 'locked inside'! What a gadabout you are!"

"That's what I told her." Marcelu smirked.

"Well, I can say for sure that I'm done for today," stated Amelia. "I need some rest."

"Go to Marcelu's room and lie in bed. I'll come to change your dressings in a few minutes," commanded Isaura.

"All right, Doctor." Amelia sighed and toddled to the bedroom.

After they were done with that rather unpleasant procedure, Marcelu brought two glasses of milkshake he had made with strawberry and peach and turned on the computer.

"What music do you like?" he asked. "I'll put something on so my parents don't overhear us."

"A bit of everything. What do you usually listen to?"

"What about Sepultura?" asked Marcelu, opening

a folder on his computer.

"Perfect."

As the rhythmic sound of thrash metal filled the room, Marcelu said, "Chicco answered. He agreed to meet with us and talk."

"Oh, really? Where is he?"

"He didn't tell me, exactly. He's afraid that his accomplices may turn him in to the police. And I believe that's very likely. So he prefers to lie low now and stay away from Lindageral. But he said I can meet him tomorrow morning in Guaratinguetá."

"Perfect. Let's drive there together."

"I'm not sure... I guess he wanted to talk to me face-to-face. I'll have to ask him if we both can be there. He's the one who can tell us what their gang was up to, and if we scare him, he'll just vanish."

Amelia sighed. "All right. Tell him that my mom is a lawyer and can help him settle all his legal troubles. And she will do it for someone who saved my life. But first, I want to hear the story from him directly."

"Okay." Marcelu took his phone and started typing a message. "I'll try to urge him to cooperate with you. But really, it's like handling a dye bag—one false move, and it explodes. He has a mind of his own, so stubborn and distrustful."

"It's good that you're the one he trusts, then," noted Amelia. She lay back in the bed and put her hands behind her neck, staring at the ceiling and pondering. "You know, I'm really bugged about that guy from the flyer, Leonardo Solas. I recall now that you saw Leon Wargas, the reporter, shooting something in our neighborhood. Could it be possible that he also worked for this Solas?"

Marcelu frowned. "I don't think he would work for anybody. He's always stated his independence."

"I know, but it must be about the election campaign. I'm almost sure." She looked at Marcelu. "Can we somehow get in touch with him?"

"Let's see." He turned to the computer and searched the journalist's name. "Here's his personal website... and there's an option to send him a message."

"Perfect!"

"So, what should we write to him?"

Amelia thought for a moment. "What about 'I am a private investigator that lives in Lindageral, and in the last two months, our quiet city has become a scene for some highly suspicious activity involving an organized criminal gang, kidnapping and killing people, and using dirty tricks to promote one of the candidates to the Chamber of Deputies. I am a big admirer of your work and think that you are the person who could figure out what's going on while the police are at a loss, and I would like to have a talk with you'?"

"Sounds solid," agreed Marcelu, and he typed it out. "All right. It was sent successfully."

"Awesome. If he doesn't answer in the next few days, I'll ask my mom to get his phone number. She used to work at the newspaper and should still have some connections left."

"We may use it, yeah." Marcelu closed the browser tab and turned to Amelia. "Are you ready to fall asleep?

Or maybe we could watch a movie together?”

“Let’s watch something,” agreed Amelia eagerly. “But only if there’s no violence or horror. I’ve had enough of that recently.”

“For sure. Have you seen *Samantha*?”

“Yes, I saw a couple of episodes at my friend’s house. It’s pretty good.”

Marcelu turned on the show on the computer and sat at the foot of the bed, making sure not to touch Amelia’s wounded leg. She smiled at his careful moves and tried to concentrate on the screen, but soon her eyelids got heavy, and she fell asleep before she knew it.

CHAPTER EIGHTEEN

"SO, WHERE ARE WE GOING?" asked Amelia as Marcelu and she got in his car after both of his parents left for work.

"Chicco sent me the coordinates where we should pick him up. It's in the suburbs of Guaratinguetá, just a ten-minute drive."

"So he doesn't mind my presence?"

"I told him we're both coming, and he didn't say anything about it. I guess that means he's okay with it."

Following the instructions of the navigator, Marcelu entered Guaratinguetá and pulled into a parking lot near a small market. He parked the car and took out his phone, intending to call Chicco, but Amelia spoke.

"There he is!" She noticed the scrawny figure of a man wearing a black baseball hat and sunglasses approaching them.

Marcelu waved to him and unlocked the doors, letting Chicco in. "Hey, mate! Nice to see you."

"Yep," agreed Chicco grumpily.

"How's everything?"

"Not too shabby."

"What are your plans, may I ask? Are you staying in Guaratingueta?"

"I'm going to get as far away from here as I can."

"Makes sense, I guess. So, can we talk?"

"Let's take a drive to the river. If you want to get roasted in this car under the sun, that's not how I want to spend my day."

"Sure. Would you mind showing me the road?"

Following Chicco's directions, they took a bridge over Paraíba do Sul river and left the city.

"Where exactly are you taking us?" asked Amelia, turning to Chicco. "I feel somewhat insecure."

"Don't worry. I have no evil intentions. I'm fully in your power now. Glad to see that you're fine, by the way," said Chicco in a toneless voice.

Amelia gave him a doubtful glance, saying nothing.

"Turn left to any driveway now," Chicco commanded Marcelu. "I'm not telling you which one so you don't think that I'm setting a trap for you."

Marcelu nodded at him in the rearview mirror and pulled off the highway to a narrow side road between thick bushes leading to the bank of the Paraíba River.

"Nice place!" said Marcelu as he parked at the end of the driveway.

"It sure is. Let's take a walk, but leave your phones in the car," demanded Chicco.

Marcelu put his device in the glove compartment, and Amelia did the same after some hesitation.

They made their way to the river.

"I met that guy, Ben, about three months ago," Chicco began. "He popped into our car service for oil change. The owner, Antonio, was in a crappy mood that day and yelled at me like crazy, so I told him to eff off. Ben heard all that, and after he left, he asked me if I would like another job. Said he was looking for a couple of capable guys. I said sure, so he set up a meeting with his boss, Jacques Costa. First, they simply offered me money to be their handyman and help with repair when needed and do dirtier jobs when needed. I refused, said I wasn't looking for any kind of trouble. Then Costa said I was a damn good mechanic and just the kind of guy they needed, who is fed up running errands for idiots who own all the money. Said they were going to serve justice to scumbags like my boss who think they are better than anyone just because they have lots of money. 'Think about it,' he said. 'You can make a real difference to how things are, besides earning enough money to open your own service and never run errands for any rich idiot.' Now, that was an offer I couldn't turn down so easily. He told me they called it the Small Business Promotion Alliance."

"This name doesn't sound very exciting," noted Amelia.

"Pretty boring, yeah," agreed Marcelu. "Nothing like a secret organization from movies, like Night Wolves or something, right?"

"First of all, they explained their mission to me," Chicco continued, "and I should say I was impressed. Of course, they asked me not to chat about it with the other guys. They didn't need to know anything besides what they were told to do, but I was supposed to be Ben's right hand, so they wanted me to have an idea. Costa began with the things I already knew—that all the money and power in our country belongs to the elite, to clans and big concerns that own it all. And for small people, it's hard to get out there, no matter how hard they work. He mentioned Antonio, who is a dumbhead, but he owns a business just because he married the daughter of a rich man. And I will never be in his position, no matter how good I am at working with my hands."

Marcelu nodded empathetically.

"And then he went on about huge corporations that own everything from diners and gas stations to huge factories. Smaller businesses, ones you or me could open, using only our skills and a loan from a bank, would never beat them.

"Those guys have all the power in their hands. They own all the money, and they have connections with authorities, police, and other huge businesses. You may call me paranoid, but you can't deny that's how things work in our country."

"Sounds very real," agreed Amelia, frowning.

"See, even you can't tell it's not true," remarked Chicco. "But they came up with a smart solution for this problem. What if the small-business owners unite in the

Alliance and help each other? Together, they can do much more than each of them alone. They can actually do more than huge corporations if the Alliance is always one step ahead.”

“So it’s something like a trade union but outlaw and undercover?” asked Marcelu.

“You could say so, yeah,” said Chicco. “Only, those unions can’t really do much. The law protects only those who have power. I totally agreed with those guys that we never win the race with major corporations if we play by their rules.”

Amelia gave him a deprecating look. “So you decided that you can just disregard any rules and laws if they don’t benefit you? Just like that?”

Chicco rolled his eyes and gave a tired sigh. “Did you even hear what I said? There were only two choices: to put up with the existing order or to bend the law.” He looked at Amelia closely. “But when they suggested I torture and kill innocent people, that was it for me. That’s a line I would never cross.”

“I’m glad to hear it,” said Amelia with genuine sympathy. “And I appreciate your help. It was you who made that anonymous call, right?”

He nodded. “When they were planning the kidnapping, it was one thing. Didn’t seem like an absolutely bad thing to me, given we would set the person free after getting what we wanted. But that time, everything was different. Those guys were so mad they would do anything. And I was fed up with them, myself, to be honest.”

Amelia looked at her feet. "Don't want to judge you. I guess you had your reasons. But can you tell me what was their reason to kidnap me? To get a ransom or what?"

"Well, I guess they could get a whole bunch of money for the only child of your wealthy father and use it to finance their activities. But as I figured out, they wanted to kill two birds with one stone."

"So, what was the second bird?" Amelia asked.

"It's kinda speculative. I'm not quite sure…" Chicco hesitated. "But I guess they wanted to arrange everything in order to frame some major figure. That's the idea I got from the conversation I overheard between Ben and Costa. But I can't remember now exactly what they said."

"Well, considering the information we have, that makes sense." Marcelu nodded.

"Yeah, I would say they wanted to pit two major players against each other. That would serve the goals of the Alliance perfectly well."

"That's so sweet, to find out that I'm just a figurehead in somebody's game," Amelia said, crossing her arms over her chest.

Marcelu embraced her by the shoulders in consolation. "So, this Jacques Costa. Is he the one in charge of the Alliance?"

Chicco shook his head. "He's the boss of Ben and a couple other guys in charge of their own gangs in the states of São Paulo, Minas Gerais, and Rio de Janeiro. But I believe there's also someone in charge of Jacques. I had an impression he didn't always know in advance what we would have to do. He received orders from someone."

"Holy Virgin, so there isn't just one gang?" Amelia blurted out.

Chicco laughed from his throat. "No, their scale is much larger than you could even imagine. They are going to spread their network throughout all Brazil."

Amelia and Marcelu looked at each other with astonishment on their faces.

"Well... I guess that's going to be the bailiwick of the Federal Police," said Marcelu.

"Bah. Good luck to them," scoffed Chicco. "You can catch one snake but not the million ants hidden underground."

"But who coordinates this network? And how do they arrange everything? What is the source of their financing?" Marcelu asked. "I believe all those raids and secret operations require some investments. Did you get paid for it?"

"Yes, and pretty good," sneered Chicco.

"So where does all this money come from?"

"As far as I know, the business owners who joined the Alliance paid their dues in an amount depending on their size and income so that it wasn't burdensome."

"Can you name the owners who you know are in the Alliance?" asked Marcelu.

Chicco smirked and shook his head. "Sorry, mate. I'm not with the Alliance anymore, but I don't like those they're sabotaging, either, and have no desire to help them."

On the way back, Chicco asked Marcelu to drop

him off a couple of blocks from the parking lot where they'd met him.

"Take good care," Marcelu told him.

"Sure. You as well."

"Do you mind if I compose a report based on what you said and submit it anonymously to the police?"

"Sure, do whatever you like as long as you don't get me into it," Chicco said before he was gone.

"Do you believe that report would help?" asked Amelia when they left Guaratingueta.

"I don't know... For sure, I will talk to my dad first and tell him everything as it is—probably without naming Chicco. I don't want to make him liable for covering up a criminal."

"We definitely need to discuss this with him and my parents. It seems to be far beyond even what they can deal with!" Amelia nervously brushed her hair with her fingers. "Do you realize what it means if Chicco is telling the truth?"

"A brand-new invisible power ruling the entire country." Marcelu nodded. "I don't think Chicco just made this up. He's a straightforward person who always tells the truth even if nobody is asking for it. That's one of the reasons he gets hated so much."

"Oh!" was all she had to say.

They kept silent all the way back.

As expected, nobody was home to notice their absence. Marcelu went to his room while Amelia took a jar with homemade lemonade from the refrigerator and poured herself a glass, adding some ice cubes. Feeling like her brain was about to explode, she sat on a couch and took a sip of the cold drink, suppressing all the questions and realizations that were popping up in her mind. It was too much to comprehend at once.

"Guess what?" asked Marcelu, entering the living room. "I've got an answer from Leon Wargas! He seems to be interested and wants to hear the details. He scheduled a video chat for us today at four p.m."

"Oh, that's great." Amelia nodded. "Actually... I just realized this. Could he also be a member of the Alliance?"

Marcelu raised his eyebrows. "Why would he join them?"

"Well, it seems like he's just that kind of person who would support their mission—a crusader for justice. He must be someone who knows all the dark sides of how things are done better than anyone."

Marcelu pondered for a moment, frowning. "Do you really think he could be one of them?"

"I don't know! That's the thing. How can we possibly know who is involved with them when our housekeeper, that innocuous old lady who was so nice to me, turned out to work for people who wanted to kidnap me for ransom?" Amelia raised her hands, at a loss.

"I see what you mean..." Marcelu nodded, a baffled expression on his face. "We need to be extra cautious in what information we feed him. Nothing except what is available to the public. And clearly, we shouldn't mention we've heard anything about the Alliance or suspect any major conspiracy."

At four in the afternoon, they both sat on chairs in front of Marcelu's computer with a prompt and a list of questions they had prepared.

Marcelu activated the call, and they saw a black-haired man in a dark-blue polo shirt and neatly trimmed beard, who examined them with an inquiring look from behind his square black-rimmed glasses.

"Good afternoon, Leon! I'm Marcelu Campras, and this is my friend and schoolmate Amelia."

She waved.

Wargas frowned as he saw her bruised face. "What happened to the young lady?"

"I... I had a very unpleasant encounter with some criminal elements recently."

Wargas nodded compassionately. "Is this related to the events Marcelu and I talked about?"

"We believe so," Marcelu said. "When such things happen in succession, it's logical to suggest a connection between them. The scum who assaulted Amelia got arrested, but they refuse to testify."

"That's too bad."

"So you are our last hope to find out the truth. I know that you and your assistants filmed a video in Lindageral a few weeks ago."

As Marcelu paused to see his reaction, Leon squinted skeptically. "I was there. Yes."

"I understand that it's most likely confidential information, but I have to ask. What was the objective of your video?"

The reporter knitted his brow. "I'd rather not bring

it up, indeed. Especially as my trip was in vain—I didn't get the material I expected to get. But it was my fault that I followed somebody's lead without checking the facts."

"So basically, somebody suggested you go to Lindageral in order to film a video that would reveal some scandalous facts?" Marcelu assumed. "And I believe that the only figure in our town who could draw the attention of an international reporter is Robert del Atore, who among other things is a candidate for the Brazilian government."

"Smart thinking." Leon's lips curved in a slight smile.

"And I believe I will not be mistaken if I suggest that the person who urged you to film the report is one of his rivals. I even daresay the name: Leonardo Solas."

Leon hesitated for a moment. "I can neither confirm nor deny that. You are smart enough to understand that it would be a huge mistake to cause a scandal around a candidate's name without solid ground. I value my reputation above anything, and I never make statements not supported by facts."

"Senhor Wargas," interrupted Amelia, "Robert del Atore is my father, and since he started his election campaign, I've been attacked twice by people who are probably connected with one of his opponents. They tried to kidnap me right after my graduation party. Then they beat me almost to death. Do you really think people who do such things should be allowed to get away with this?"

Leon's face fell. "No, I don't think so. I'm definitely taking the case."

"We're not asking you for the names, but maybe

you could share the details of your trip with us?" asked Marcelu.

Leon leaned back in his chair, putting his hands behind his head and thought for a moment. "I was informed that while Robert del Atore is running for the government position, his hometown is in absolute devastation, roads haven't been repaired for decades, and all public facilities are a complete wreckage."

Amelia gasped in indignation. "That's not true!"

"I know. I've been there. Also, I was told that workers on plantations belonging to del Atore are facing severe violations of terms of employment. That they hire minors who work over the hours allowable and that the workers are not getting paid on time. But I talked to a couple of people, and they said that while they had some incidents about five years ago, now both seasonal and permanent workers have decent wages and labor conditions."

Amelia nodded eagerly. "There was a manager who abused his authority. My parents were too busy with the machinery business in São Paulo at that time. There was a crisis that required their attention, and that man took advantage of the lack of oversight. But when he was replaced with a more suitable person, things got much better."

"That's what I heard," Leon confirmed. "I was expected to interview one of the local business owners who was very upset with the situation in the town. But at the very last moment, he changed his mind and refused to talk."

"Was his name Marinio Risso, by any chance?" Marcelu guessed. "He was killed on the next day after your visit," he explained as the reporter looked at him with his mouth agape.

"Holy Virgin! Yes, him. I had no idea he got killed. Can you give me more details about that case?"

Marcelu informed him of all the facts he knew.

"Thank you for sharing this," Wargas finally said. "I still can't reveal my sources to you, but I'm going to start my own investigation as soon as I can. Tomorrow afternoon, I'm heading to Lindageral."

CHAPTER NINETEEN

"WHAT DO YOU THINK ABOUT RISSO'S murder now?" asked Amelia when they went to the kitchen for a snack. "It looks like he was the one of the Alliance clients."

"Yeah, all the signs are there. Obviously, he got out of their control, and that's why they killed him," said Marcelu, opening a box of cookies.

"I don't believe Elvina had anything to do with this, though. Do you?" asked Amelia.

"No, I don't think so. She wouldn't tell us about her suspicions regarding her father's contacts if she was involved."

Amelia took a bite of cookie and chewed it mechanically, processing all the overwhelming information. "Here's the thing," she said finally. "We need to look for small business owners who all of the sudden became very successful and had an increase in income.”

Marcelu rubbed his lips thoughtfully. “I guess it’s not so easy to get this data in real time. In theory, we can get the information from the revenue agency, but only after they process all the declarations. If the Alliance started its activity only last year, we could see the earliest information in half a year. This year has just started.”

“That’s at least some clue… But half a year is a long time.” Amelia disheveled her hair, thinking intensely. “Bingo! I think I know a better way!” she finally gushed. “We need to question accountants. Remember Elvina’s accountant, Camilla, mentioned that she worked with almost a hundred small businesses? They must be aware of such changes.”

“I think accountants are a cautious folk,” noted Marcelu. “I’m not sure they will be eager to give away their owners’ secrets.”

“That’s true too. We need to know how to fish for this information.”

“What if we ask Camilla for help? She’s Elvina’s friend, and I’m sure she would want to help us bring all the people involved in his death to justice. And she probably knows other accountants and could get information from them in an unobtrusive manner.”

Marcelu pondered her words. “Maybe… But we need to think everything through and be very careful what we say.”

“That’s for sure! To start with, we could simply talk to her and ask if she has any fellow accountants to recommend to us and then see where the conversation goes and how cooperative she will be.”

“Well, I guess it’s worth a shot,” Marcelu agreed after some hesitation. “But I think it’s better to discuss it with my father first.”

“Don’t get me wrong, but I don’t think that’s a good idea. Your father may want to interrogate her, and talking to a police officer would stress anyone out and kill any initiative to cooperate. Yes, I know your dad is a nicest policeman ever, but he’s still a policeman,” added Amelia, noticing Marcelu inhaling to say something. “People are afraid of them. She knows that we are friendly and would feel safer with us.”

“Fine.” Marcelu sighed.

“Do you have Camilla’s number?”

“No, but I can ask Elvina for it.”

Marcelu took his phone and quickly typed a message. The answer followed in a minute.

“Here we go.”

“Excellent. I’ll call her.”

Amelia stretched out her hand, and Marcelu passed the phone to her. She clicked and dialed the highlighted number.

“Hi, Camilla! It’s Amelia, Amelia del Atore. We met at Elvina’s place. Yes, how are you doing today? Great! I just wanted to ask if we could meet with you anytime soon. My family needs help from a professional accountant with some delicate problem, and I would like to discuss it with you confidentially. You helped Camilla in her complicated case, and you are the one we can trust with this issue. I know that you're busy, but if you could give us some advice or recommend one of your colleagues, that would be awesome."

Marcelu gave her a thumbs up.

"Yes, sure. I don't have much to do anyway. Perfect. See you soon!" Amelia ended the call and resumed, "Camilla is home tonight and said I can come by anytime."

"Do you want to go right now?" asked Marcelu reluctantly.

"Sure. There's no reason to delay it. Her address is twenty-three Rua de Santa Catarina. How far is that? Can we take a walk?"

"It's quite far. It would take about forty minutes to walk. And you are not supposed to be seen by anyone, so we'll take a car."

"Let's go, then!"

Camilla's house was one of the last on a street of well-kept cottages drowning in lush green stretched along Paraíba do Sul.

"It's there!" Amelia pointed at a gate in a solid wooden fence with a metallic golden number 23 on it.

"Neat home," noted Marcelu as he parked the car on the curb. "Looks like accounting is a good way to make money."

"I guess so, if you aren't lazy."

Amelia knocked at the gate, and in a minute, Camilla appeared, to let them in. She looked quite unusual wearing wide shorts, a loose T-shirt, a straw fedora, and rubber slippers instead of the businesslike outfit they'd seen on her before.

"Hi! Come in, please!" She smiled widely at them. "Sorry, I was working in the garden, so I'm all covered in mud."

"No worries, and thanks for finding time for us," said Amelia.

Camilla led them inside the modern style house with huge windows.

"Would you like to have a cup of tea on the patio?" she asked.

"Sure," Amelia said.

Camilla washed her hands of dirt in the kitchen sink, turned on the kettle, showed her guests the way through the sliding glass door to the backyard patio with a round glass table with rattan chairs, and soon joined them with two cups of tea.

"You have such a nice place," noted Amelia, looking at the well-kept garden with blueberry bushes and flower beds.

"Thank you. I was glad to find a quiet and peaceful corner like this, where my mom would feel good."

"How is your mom doing?" Amelia asked.

Camilla sighed. "She is not very well lately. Actually, I had to take her to a private care facility because she needs care I am not able to provide her myself, as I am too busy with work."

Amelia nodded empathetically. "That's sad."

"By the way, if you like this neighborhood, the third house on my side was just put up for rent, in case you're looking for a place to live together," said Camilla with a slight smile.

"Um... We're not..." stuttered Amelia.

"We're not ready for this yet," finished Marcelu. "I'm going to São Paulo to study at the university next month."

"Ah, good for you! So, you said you were looking for an accountant?" she asked Amelia.

"Yes. Basically, one of the affiliates of Campoverde, our company, had a whole deal of troubles with its accountant. He stole money and ran away, leaving a huge mess. So we need someone who'd be able to deal with it. I know you already are too busy, but maybe you could recommend someone reliable?"

Camilla raised her eyebrows. "Oh, that's too bad! I need to think about who could be fit for this work."

"It's so hard to find a good accountant nowadays," lamented Amelia. "I even started to think about becoming an accountant myself. I could work at our family company or even start my own business and be sure that nobody is sabotaging it."

"Very wise thought," remarked Camilla.

"By the way, you're probably the one who knows what types of businesses make more money—franchises, big retail chains, or independent owners, if we're talking about consumer goods retail or restaurants?"

"That's an interesting question." Camilla thought for a moment. "I would say chain companies have some advantage, but it really depends on many factors."

Amelia elaborated on her tale. "I had an argument with my parents. They said if I want to open my own clothes store, it's better to start by joining a retail chain or I risk having all my investments go up in smoke. But I'm sure there are independent businesses who are doing very well. Maybe you know some?"

"You want to gather statistics to persuade your parents?" Camilla grinned.

"Basically, yes." Amelia smiled back at her. "Maybe you could give me some stats?"

"I'll see what I can do," Camilla answered. "So where are you planning to open your store? In Lindageral?"

"I'm trying to figure out if it will be profitable to have it here. Maybe you could help me with numbers..."

They heard a loud and persistent knock on the gate.

"Excuse me." Camilla stood up and went to answer.

"Good story, but don't get too carried away," said Marcelu in a lowered tone when they were alone.

"I know. At least she didn't say no, so a little bit more persuasion, and maybe it will work out."

Through the open back door, they heard a demanding man arguing about something with Camilla. The voices got more distinct as they entered the house.

"I tell you, there's nothing I can do for you. Really!" said Camilla.

"Listen, the boss told me to get the money from you and get lost till the cops got to me. You better obey."

"Rubbish!" Camilla scoffed. "He didn't tell you so."

Amelia froze with her mouth agape. "Oh my, it's him! Ben!" She quietly got up from the table, and as she backed away from the glass panel covered by curtains, she gestured for Marcelu to follow her behind the corner of the building where they couldn't be seen from inside.

"Well, *I* am telling you, and you'd better not piss me off! Costa told me you're the one who keeps all the bank. And I need money now, to disappear for a while."

"Costa! He'd tell you anything to save his ass."

"It didn't help him either way," spat Ben. "Hey, sSis, I told you what I want—two hundred thousand reais, and we call it quits. I don't really care about anything else."

"Are you sure?" Marcelu mouthed.

Amelia nodded energetically.

"That's quite a lump! Do you think I keep such amounts of money at home? How am I supposed to get it right now?" Camilla's voice trembled.

Marcelu squatted and typed something on his silenced phone. He showed Amelia the screen with the message to the contact "Dad." She nodded in approval.

"Do you think I'm an idiot?" Ben boomed angrily. "I know very well you have it."

"What do we do now?" Amelia whispered under her breath.

Marcelu waved a hand in a warning gesture and mouthed, "Wait!"

"All right, fine, just let me find the keys to my safe."

For the next few minutes, they heard only indistinct noises then a loud *pop* and a *thud* of something falling on the floor. They both froze for a moment. Marcelu stood up and carefully peeked into the window then rushed to the door. Amelia followed him.

Ben was lying on the floor of the living room with a bloodstain on his T-shirt expanding from a wound on the left side of his chest, his body shuddering. Something flickered in his eyes when he saw Amelia, and his lips moved, but the sound that left them was a muffled rattle as his wide-open eyes glazed. His body shuddered one more time and went still.

Amelia switched her gaze to Camilla, who seemed to be stunned as well, holding a gun with a silencer in her lowered hand.

"I had to protect myself..." she muttered. "He would've killed me. He asked me for money I didn't have."

"Is he dead?" Amelia looked at the body on the floor in horror.

Marcelu knelt and tried to palpate a jugular vein in the man's neck. "Yes," he said with dismay on his face. "There's a gun in his pocket," he noted, pointing at Ben's unzipped jacket.

"Don't touch anything," Amelia warned him automatically.

Marcelu stood up and addressed Camilla. "What business did you have with these guys?"

"They asked me to do some accounting for them." Camilla wiped sweat from her forehead with her hand.

"Why did you never bring it up when Elvina talked about that man with a spider tattoo, Jaques Costa?" Marcelu frowned. "It seems that you knew him."

"I know way too many people because of my work, and not all of them are nice. My rule is 'Don't ask. Don't tell.' I don't want any trouble. My mother is sick, and I am the only person who can take care of her," said Camilla, breathing heavily.

"Did you do accounting for the Alliance?" asked Amelia.

Camilla gave her an odd look. "The Alliance?"

Afraid that she'd said too much, Amelia turned to Marcelu, who gave her a warning look. "I mean for this gang."

"I might have done some paperwork for them. You see, they are hard to get away from."

"All right, it's not our business to question you," said Marcelu, succumbing. "Have a seat, please. You need to calm down."

"Sorry. I need some fresh air." She headed to the back door, still holding the gun.

"Wait!" Marcelu stood in her way. "How did you know he was lying when he said something about what their boss told him? Do you know who the boss is?"

Camilla grabbed his hand, jerked it abruptly, and hit him in the temple with the grip of the gun. He fell on the floor.

"Marcelu!" screamed Amelia. She took a step forward and stumbled as Camilla pointed the gun at her.

"Hush now!" she commanded. "I don't know about you, but I don't want more dead bodies in this house."

"What are you doing?" whispered Amelia. "We don't want any harm to you."

"Very well. Open that drawer and get the duct tape." Camilla pointed at a drawer under the counter. "Now bind his feet and arms," she commanded as Amelia picked up the roll of tape with a dispenser.

Amelia obeyed, slowly knelt on the floor, and wrapped tape around the ankles and wrists of Marcelu, who was stunned and showed no protest.

"Hope that will keep you from sticking your nose in my business for a while," Camilla said as Amelia finished. "You, out!" she commanded, nodding toward the back door.

At gunpoint, Amelia proceeded through the nicely trimmed garden to a gate at the back, opening to the river, where a shabby fishing powerboat floated, locked to a pillar of a wooden dock with a chain.

CHAPTER TWENTY

"GET IN THE BOAT!" ORDERED CAMILLA. Amelia climbed onboard, and Camilla followed her, grabbed onto the gunwale with her left hand, and shot the lock off the chain. Amelia fell back, stunned by the muffled—but still loud—sound and leaned against the transom. Camilla took one of two seats, put the gun on the dashboard, and started the engine. The boat pulled away and dashed through the waves. Camilla pulled closer to the opposite bank and headed down the stream at breathtaking speed. Crouched behind her, Amelia reminded herself that at least Marcelu was safe and his father had gotten his message and would soon be there to release him. And if Camilla had wanted to kill her, she probably would have done it already...

When they left Lindageral behind, Camilla reduced

the speed so the roar of the engine wasn't as loud.

Amelia pulled herself up to her knees, holding onto the backrest of the seat next to the driver. "Hey, do you mind telling me what's going on?" she asked. "I mean, it's still not too late! It's not a big deal even if you had something to do with those guys. I understand that you just were afraid. And with Ben, it was obvious self-defense. No need to panic and run!"

Camilla turned to her and laughed. Wind disheveled her hair, and her eyes sparkled. Nothing was left of her usual mask of well-mannered reserve.

"You're so funny, Senhorita Amelia! I'm not panicking. I don't want to waste my time on explanations with idiots. I have a whole Alliance to run."

"How do you run it?" Amelia felt dizzy and disoriented, as if she'd been spinning for too long.

"As well as I can, obviously." Camilla laughed again. "Don't think that anybody will manage it better, though, as it's my brainchild."

Amelia stared at her in utter dismay.

"Frustrating, isn't it? Even if you tell someone, hardly anyone would take you seriously."

"Why would you do this?" Amelia couldn't help asking, hating how stupid her question sounded.

"Why?" Camilla glanced at her. "Because someone has to deal with the wrongs of this world. *Ordem e Progresso*, right? I didn't have an option to have a normal life anyway."

"Why?" Amelia repeated. The green banks flickering past the boat made her nauseated, so she focused on Camilla's face instead.

"I happened to be born to a maniac who terrorized people in three different states. Who almost burnt my mother alive just to prove he could do anything with her."

"That's terrible... I hope he's in jail now."

Camilla scoffed. "Jail is not for people like Amarillio del Atore." She turned to see Amelia's reaction and couldn't hold back her laughter at seeing Amelia's stunned face.

"Yes, my father was an infamous psychopath, and my mother is one of his playthings. I guess the fact that she was his son's wife heated him even more."

Amelia needed a while to process what she'd heard. "You mean... my dad's wife? Your mom...? Senhora Dolores?"

"She was called Priscilla Resende back then."

"She can't be! She died, that woman... Priscilla. I saw it in the newspaper!"

"Oh, so you heard that story? How sweet. Yes and no. She survived, but she never was as before. She got injuries she barely survived, lost her pregnancy, and developed a severe mental disorder. Amarillio decided to spare her at the very last moment—or maybe he planned this from the start. You can never tell a psychopath's mind."

Amelia put her head in her hands. "Why didn't she reach out to my dad if she was alive?" she screamed in a desperate attempt to shatter Camilla's story.

"She was afraid Amarillio would kill them both, I guess. She's lived in a permanent state of terror ever since, my mom, as long as I've known her."

"That's horrible..."

Camilla nodded. "When I was a little girl, life seemed pretty good to me. We lived in a nice home in São Paulo suburbia, mostly just me and my mom, but Father popped up from time to time and brought me cool toys and dresses. Only Mom wasn't happy to see him. I saw her crying each time after he left. When I went to school, Mom forbade me from telling anyone who my dad was. I didn't even know his last name anyway. I was fourteen when I found out the real state of things. To put it simply, I was outraged and decided I wouldn't put up with it. I persuaded my mom to move to another address, and I called Amarillio and told him my mom's story would be on all the news channels in Brazil and the whole world if he didn't do what I said. I had enough proof, and I was so furious that I wasn't able to feel any fear. I was ready to die but not retreat."

"And?" asked Amelia impatiently when Camilla ran out of breath and stopped.

Camilla nodded. "He sold his share in Campoverde and transferred sixty-six percent to my mother's account—enough for us to never worry about money. Surely, he sold it to an outsider just to spite his son. I knew that when I traced the transaction to make sure we got what he promised."

"Really? That's cool!" admitted Amelia with awe.

Camilla smirked. "I guess I was the biggest mistake he ever made."

"But now you've become someone who terrorizes

people.”

“That’s not my aim, you know. Think about it, and you’ll understand. You’re not that spoiled rich girl I thought you would be. I even came to like you.”

“Was it you who tried to steal the invention my dad is working with? Our housekeeper, Theresa... Was she one of yours?”

“I’m not answering such questions,” Camilla retorted. “But yes, I have my people everywhere.”

“But why? My father is working on a project that can benefit our country. Isn’t that what you want as well?”

Camilla leered at her. “Seriously? Benefit the country by helping major tycoons like Lacerdo and Carvalho get richer? I would find a better way to do it, giving a chance to smaller companies. I don’t have anything against your father personally, but he’s a part of a corrupt system.”

Amelia shook her head. “Look what it all led to! Risso is dead. How many more people have or will die?”

“It wasn’t planned. I didn’t want to harm anyone. I’ve used the wrong people this time, but I will learn from my mistakes.”

“How can you be sure that things won’t just get worse? How can you keep everything under control?”

“Enough questions! Get out.” Camilla pulled closer to the bank and slowed down.

“What?” Amelia asked at a loss.

“I said it’s your stop. Off you pop,” said Camilla impatiently. “It’s shallow enough. You can walk to shore.”

Not willing to tempt her fate, Amelia climbed

overboard and plunged into the water, which reached the middle of her chest. The sun was setting, and the brown waters of Paraíba turned dark orange and red in its rays. After Amelia took a few steps away, Camilla roared off, stirring a wave that softly pushed at her. She plodded to the grassy shore and waded through bushes to see what seemed like endless grassland and hills with no signs of any settlement where she could get any help. Dusk was falling, and she had no money, no phone, and no idea of her location besides the left shore of Paraíba do Sul. As water ran down from her jeans and squelched in her runners, she walked through the meadows as fast as her wounded leg allowed her till she ended up on a road that brought her to a village, where she scared some local kids kicking a ball on a side road, who thought she was a ghost. Their parents made her a cup of tea, offered dinner, which she refused, and gave her a phone to make a call after she explained she'd become a victim of some scoundrels that kidnapped her and pushed from a boat. She didn't go into all the details.

Marcelu didn't answer her call. She sent him a message that she was safe and soon would be home, hoping that he was well. The lady that borrowed the phone to her offered to call their neighbor who was offering occasional car service. Amelia agreed, and he arrived in about ten minutes.

"Lindageral? That would be quite pricey," commented the driver, looking at her with suspicion.

"That's not a problem. I'm having an emergency, and I need to get there as soon as possible."

"Do you even have money?"

"Nothing with me—I just got robbed—but I'll pay you and give a good tip when I get home."

Grudgingly, the driver agreed and headed to Lindageral. During the trip, he tried to pry into what had happened, but Amelia held him off. Not capable of talking or thinking, she simply stared out the window, telling herself that everything was going to end and she would see Marcelu very soon.

"Thank goodness, Amelia!" Isaura called to her as she popped out of her home when the car stopped near their gate.

"I'm fine, Isaura! What's up with Marcelu?"

"He's fine. He's home," Isaura said, gently hugging her.

"I need to pay the driver."

"Just go inside. I'll take care of it."

"Amelia!" gasped Marcelu as she entered the living room.

She beamed. "You're safe!"

He approached her, and she took him in a warm embrace.

"What happened? Did you escape?" asked Marcelu, looking down at her wet jeans.

"Camilla let me go. She ran away on a boat. She told me..." Her voice failed her, and she dropped her face into her palm.

"That's all right. You need to change and get some rest. Everything else can wait," Marcelu said in a soothing tone.

The next morning as they sat in the garden, Lucrecia said, "Yes, young people, you found out what nobody else even expected." She'd come to check up on her daughter as soon as she could after she got the news while Robert was in São Paulo on business. "I would say kudos, but I don't want to encourage your reckless behavior. You both nearly got killed!"

"Sorry, Mom, but who could've imagined that visiting Camilla Soares would be a risky venture?" Amelia objected.

"Right." Lucrecia shook her head. "I hope the police will do their best to find her."

"Yes, the police are looking for her with regard to the murder of Benedito Moraes, the mercenary gang leader, but you know, a good accountant is hard to find." Marcelu smirked. "I bet she prepared an escape plan for any outcome." He patted Princess Celestia, who sat at his feet.

Lucrecia scoffed. "Smart bugger!"

"I told my father all the information we got regarding the Alliance, but he says it would hardly be taken seriously, based just on an anonymous report and Amelia's and my testimonies. But if there are more attacks on well-known companies, they will bring it up and take it seriously."

"If I got it right from what you said, they were up to much more than just sabotaging the businesses they did not approve of. They used all means to promote their candidate to the Deputies' Chamber. I always knew there was something wrong with that Leonardo Solas!"

"It seems very plausible that he's Camilla's puppet," said Marcelu. "Her ambitions are far from modest."

"And of course we'd never be able to prove anything." Lucrecia pursed her lips. "But at least we can take this revelation into account in our further actions."

"It's good to be forewarned," noted Marcelu. "All right, if you excuse me, I guess I should take my dog for a walk." He pushed Princess Celestia's paws off his lap.

"How do I tell your father that his first wife is still alive?" Lucrecia asked rhetorically when the two of them were left alone.

"That's quite the news, I know. Not only alive but also gave birth to his sister, who wants to sabotage his business and career. Poor Dad. That would be too much for him."

"Poor Dad?" spat Lucrecia. "What about poor me? I am the one who should be worried. I wasn't ready to discover after twenty years that my marriage is illegitimate. What am I worth without it? A forty-year-old woman who hasn't built any solid career because she was too busy working as a public relations manager for her husband—who's turned out to be another woman's husband now."

Amelia raised her eyebrows in surprise. "Seriously, Mom? I saw that woman. The last thing she would want is to take Dad away from you. And I guess, as she has a legally different identity, your marriage is still legal. Even if it's not, who cares? It's a free country, thank goodness."

"That's not the case." Lucrecia bit her lip. "I'm sure your dad will want to do something about it. He can't just leave it as it is."

"For sure, I think he could try to find her and offer his help. That would be the right thing to do. But why would he leave you? None of this is your fault at all. And I'm sure Dad loves you more than anyone in the universe."

Lucrecia stood up and hugged her around the shoulders.

"Thank you, sweetheart. Be sure we both love you more than anyone."

"And so do I." Amelia covered her mother's hands with her palms. "And I'm sure that even if you weren't his wife anymore, you would be just as successful on your own. You're a good PR manager, after all."

"I guess you're right." Lucrecia smiled, regaining her composure. "I should think about returning to my legal practice after the election campaign. What about you and our plans regarding the college in London?"

"Well, you know, after this all happened, I started thinking that I would like to know more about all the business-related processes and money flows," said Amelia tentatively.

"That's a good idea!" Lucrecia said, somewhat surprised. "You could study economic science."

Amelia nodded. "I believe they have a course at the University of São Paulo, so I wouldn't need to go very far."

"I hope it's not because of some guy who's going to

study there?" Lucrecia winked at her.

"Mom!" Amelia protested but forgot what she wanted to say when she saw Marcelu approaching them, accompanied by Fortunata, who had a tourist backpack on her shoulder.

"Hey there!" she greeted them and frowned as she saw Amelia's bruised face.

"Sorry, Amelia. With all this mess, I forgot to tell you that your friend called me back last night," said Marcelu. "She said she would come to get her motorcycle herself, so I gave her the address."

"Amelia?" Fortunata raised her eyebrow. "So, you're not Paola, then? And what happened to you?" She was looking at her bruises.

"I will explain everything, but it may take some time. Glad to see you here!" Amelia stood up and hugged her friend. "Mom, this is Fortunata. She was so kind and sheltered me when I was in Itajubá," she explained to Lucrecia, who seemed perplexed.

"Actually, I'm here mostly because of you, not the motorcycle," Fortuna said. "I wanted to say sorry. You were right about Raul."

"What has he done now?"

"I have no idea what's going on with him since he got arrested, and I don't want to know. I was so afraid to lose him, but when I could think about it clearly, I felt like I was set free. I no longer care about him, and it feels amazing. Just like I was born again."

"That's awesome!" Amelia beamed at her.

"I decided to finally leave Itajubá, to leave no

chance that he would ever cross my path again. And your Lindageral looks like a nice place to live.”

“You want to stay here? That’s great!”

“Yes, I’m absolutely positive! Do you know any places for rent here?”

“I’m sure we will find you something.” Amelia turned to her mother. “Mom, can my friend stay at our house till she finds a place to live?”

“Of course.” Lucrecia smiled benevolently. “That’s what friends are for.”

www.ingramcontent.com/pod-product-compliance
Lightning Source LLC
Chambersburg PA
CBHW071542030726
47598CB00001B/192